KV-446-331

…AL MESSAGE TO READERS

This book is published under the auspices of

THE ULVERSCROFT FOUNDATION

(registered charity No. 264873 UK)

Established in 1972 to provide funds for research, diagnosis and treatment of eye diseases. Examples of contributions made are: —

A Children's Assessment Unit at Moorfield's Hospital, London.

•

Twin operating theatres at the Western Ophthalmic Hospital, London.

•

A Chair of Ophthalmology at the Royal Australian College of Ophthalmologists.

•

The Ulverscroft Children's Eye Unit at the Great Ormond Street Hospital For Sick Children, London.

You can help further the work of the Foundation by making a donation or leaving a legacy. Every contribution, no matter how small, is received with gratitude. Please write for details to:

THE ULVERSCROFT FOUNDATION,
The Green, Bradgate Road, Anstey,
Leicester LE7 7FU, England.
Telephone: (0116) 236 4325

In Australia write to:

THE ULVERSCROFT FOUNDATION,
c/o The Royal Australian and New Zealand
College of Ophthalmologists,
94-98 Chalmers Street, Surry Hills,
N.S.W. 2010, Australia

DALTON

Bushwhacked by corrupt lawman Walker Dodge, Dalton loses his money, his horse, his gun and very nearly his life. He recovers in the dead-end town of Harmony and hears rumours of treasure hidden nearby. Taking a risk in staying, he is enticed by Misty Valdez, who claims to know where the treasure is located. But the price of her help may be too high. With time running out, can he avoid Misty's trap and find the treasure before the gun-toting Walker catches up with him?

ED LAW

DALTON

Complete and Unabridged

LINFORD
Leicester

First published in Great Britain in 2005 by
Robert Hale Limited
London

First Linford Edition
published 2006
by arrangement with
Robert Hale Limited
London

British Library CIP Data

Law, Ed
Dalton.—Large print ed.—
Linford western library
1. Western stories
2. Large type books
I. Title
823.9′2 [F]

ISBN 1–84617–168–7

Published by
F. A. Thorpe (Publishing)
Anstey, Leicestershire

Set by Words & Graphics Ltd.
Anstey, Leicestershire
Printed and bound in Great Britain by
T. J. International Ltd., Padstow, Cornwall

This book is printed on acid-free paper

1

'Damn you to hell for all eternity!' Patrick Williams roared as he glared up at the cross.

'Yeah,' he continued. 'You heard me. I despise you. I've had enough. I am a blasphemer. And I don't care.'

Patrick turned and stormed back and forth, slamming his fist against his thigh and taking deep breaths.

The wind howled through the church's open doorway. A stray autumn leaf danced over the rows of empty pews, lodged in Patrick's long robes a moment before slamming into the boarded window above the altar. On the wall beside the boarded window, a headless depiction of Jesus confronted him, this defilement the latest in the long series of desecrations that Walker Dodge had inflicted on this small stone church.

Patrick swung to a standstill and shook a fist at the cross.

'I have done everything you wanted me to do, but you've given me nothing. I've endured five years of agony, but nobody in Harmony wants to open their hearts to your message. They only care about the food that I give them. I am nothing. And you made me nothing.'

Patrick swung round to face the door to his quarters. He took a long pace towards it, then turned back.

'Why should I ruin my life? Why should I watch people destroy others who are less worthy than themselves just because you died for my sins? Well, you can't answer that one, and this is the end.' Patrick waggled a finger. 'And if you know me, you know I mean it. So unless you help me before I've counted to ten, I'm turning my back on you, forever.'

Patrick slammed his hands on his hips and counted to five.

'Five more seconds,' he roared. 'Then

I go into that room and when I come out, I'll be finished with you.'

Patrick resumed his steady count, raising his voice so that by the time he reached ten, phlegm was showering from his mouth and he'd flexed his throat muscles into tight cords.

As the last echoes of his roared 'ten' faded to oblivion, he cupped an ear, listening to the wind whistling through the door.

'Just as I thought,' he whispered, his gruff tone sarcastic after his prolonged shouting. He turned and paced towards his room. 'You don't even exist. You — '

'Help me.'

The demand came from behind and in bemusement, Patrick swirled round.

A man leaned on the open church door, his brow bloodied, his clothes tattered and streaked with filth. The man opened his mouth again, but only a tortured moan escaped his lips.

In confusion, Patrick edged forward a pace as the man stretched out a hand to him. Then the man released his hold on the door. He stumbled and slid to the floor to lay slumped in the doorway, then rolled on to his back.

'Help me,' he whispered again, his fevered eyes closing.

* * *

'How are you feeling?' Patrick asked.

It was an hour since the man's unexpected arrival, during which time Patrick had dragged him into the church and positioned him before the altar, then used his limited knowledge of medicine to tend to his wounds.

Luckily, aside from the numerous cuts and bruises mottling the man's back and sides, Patrick found no life-threatening problems. He guessed that exhaustion had caused the man's distress rather than anything else.

So, after a whispered and apologetic conversation with the cross, he'd returned to praying until the man had begun to stir.

'I feel rough,' the man croaked. He

shuffled his position to lie on his back, then winced and rolled back on to his side. 'Is this Rock Ridge?'

'No, Harmony. Rock Ridge is fifty miles east.'

The man glanced at the altar. 'A church?'

'Yes. And I am Patrick Williams.'

'Reverend Williams, Father Williams?'

Patrick glanced up at the cross, then forced a weak smile.

'Just Patrick. But what happened to you?'

'I had me some bad luck.' The man stared over Patrick's shoulder at the wall.

Patrick clasped his hands together and widened his smile.

'It's all right. I am a man of . . . ' Patrick sighed. 'I am a man of God. I don't care who you are or what you were doing. My only concern is that you have a need. You don't even have to give me your name.'

'Suppose I don't.' The man stared at

the wall a moment longer, then roved his gaze down to Patrick. 'This bunch of varmints bushwhacked me on the trail to Rock Ridge. A man who claimed to be the law led them, but he ain't like any lawman I've ever met.'

Patrick snorted. 'That is a familiar story. Sheriff Walker Dodge reckons he can do as he pleases.'

'So he *was* a lawman,' the man mused as he raised his eyebrows. 'He reckoned I'd stolen something, but he wouldn't tell me what it was and when I didn't have what he was searching for, he stole my horse, my gun, and the few dollars I had.'

'Again, that is a familiar story.'

'Then he tied me to my own horse and dragged me down the trail. I reckon he'd have ripped me to hell, but the ground wore through the rope first and it broke. I tumbled into a river and stayed face down for as long as I could, playing dead. Walker blasted a few shots at me, then gave up.' The man shrugged. 'Then I swam to the side and followed this dry gully until I ended up here.'

'It sounds as if you were the last to suffer from Walker's latest jaunt.' Patrick let a wide smile emerge as another piece of what just had to be his 'sign' slotted into place. 'I suppose someone was looking out for you or you'd have died.'

'Suppose I was lucky. Is Walker still around?'

'He comes and goes as he pleases, but for now he isn't around. But in a week, maybe two, he will return.' Patrick patted the man's shoulder. 'But I'll ensure you're well and on your way by then.'

'I run from no man.' The man slammed a fist into his other palm, but winced when the effort rocked him to the side.

'Perhaps you don't. But sometimes not being around doesn't force you to do anything.'

Patrick stared at the man until he received a reluctant nod. Then he paced to the altar and knelt. With his hands clasped, he looked up at the cross and began a low benediction.

'Dalton.'

Patrick glanced over his shoulder. 'Sorry?'

'You didn't ask. But my name is Dalton.'

'Just Dalton?'

'Just Dalton.'

2

Although the lacerations and bruising on his back and sides were deep and sore, Dalton reckoned that Patrick's assessment was correct and his injuries weren't that severe. His ten-mile walk to Harmony had weakened him the most.

So, for the rest of the day he took advantage of Patrick's generosity and rested. But as he was too sore to find a comfortable posture to sleep, the rest only tired him even more.

In the evening, a woman who introduced herself as Verna Bunch entered the church with her husband, Milo, in tow. She was weather-hardened and angular and of that indefinable age that many in this area possessed. As she cooked a stew, the greasy-haired Milo peered at Dalton with sullen indifference.

In a side room to the left of the altar, Verna served her meal, but neither she nor Milo joined Dalton in conversation and as Dalton was fighting a losing battle against his fatigue, he welcomed the silence.

After clearing away the plates, Patrick led Verna into the church to pray while Milo wandered off. Patrick didn't ask Dalton to join them, but even if he was minded to, Dalton was already laying his head on his arms and within moments, sleep overcame his numerous aches.

Some time later a kindly hand on his shoulder awakened him. Verna had gone, although he heard movement nearby and he guessed she was close. In the corner of the room, Patrick had laid out a blanket and with gratitude Dalton crawled under it.

Even before Patrick had reached his own room, Dalton was already snoozing.

Later, he awoke and heard Patrick praying in the main church and he heard another voice, perhaps a woman's, although it wasn't Verna's.

The domestic arrangements Dalton saw and heard around him intrigued him, but he was too tired to stay awake long enough to investigate and returned to his sleep.

In the morning, after Verna had fed him, Dalton was already feeling far fitter than when he'd staggered into the church yesterday.

Even so when Patrick and Verna left on what they said were their daily rounds of administering to the town orphans and the needy, Dalton walked gingerly around the church.

The building was stone built, but whichever missionary group had felt this effort to be worthwhile had long since realized that the ramshackle town of Harmony would never amount to much and had abandoned it. The crumbling stone building had two side rooms. In Dalton's room, only one whole cupboard remained in a tangle of broken furniture, suggesting that once the building had contained relics, but they had all been looted.

Dalton resisted the temptation to explore Patrick's room.

Outside, at the front of the church, a small annex jutted out beside the door. Dalton reckoned this was where Verna and Milo had slept.

On the other side of the door someone had started building a second annex, but so far it only had one three foot high wall. And from the huge pile of rocks nearby Dalton reckoned that the work was on-going. And from the blankets piled beside the wall Dalton guessed that sometimes other people slept here, but with winter coming fast, Dalton didn't envy them.

With his tour complete, Dalton looked from the church towards Harmony. The church was a hundred yards beyond the town's edge. But Dalton judged that there was nothing to interest him in Harmony's dozen or so buildings and that he'd wandered enough for his first journey, so he headed back into the church.

He sat on the pew nearest the altar, then lay on it, and with nothing else to do, he fell into another fitful sleep.

He guessed two or three hours had passed when Patrick clumped into the church and awoke him. Patrick knelt beside Dalton and appraised his bandages. With much nodding, he declared his healing to be progressing well.

'I got nothing to pay you,' Dalton said when Patrick stood back.

Patrick shook his head. 'I never asked for anything.'

'Even so. I needed help and you were here.'

'Then we were both fortunate,' Patrick murmured. He glanced up at the cross and when he spoke again his voice was more assured. 'Yes. That is why I am here. And whenever I doubt that for a moment, someone will always have a need that only I can satisfy.'

Dalton nodded. 'Obliged. Are many people staying here? I saw the blankets in the annex at the front.'

'Sometimes the town orphans, and

sometimes other people with a need such as yours stop by, and I do my best.' Patrick smiled. 'I hope that maybe one day I can finish building the annex and provide a more permanent shelter for such people in need, especially children.'

'How long have you been working on it?'

'Two years.'

'You need to hurry.' Dalton rolled his feet to the ground and stretched, finding that his short sleep had again reduced his aches and pains. 'I was heading to Rock Ridge. If it's only fifty miles, I can walk there, but does a stage stop in Harmony?'

'No.' Patrick shrugged. 'But Chase Valdez buys in supplies and you might be able to travel out when that next happens.'

'But from the sound of your voice, you don't reckon that's any time soon.' Dalton watched Patrick shake his head. 'So I need to earn me some money while I wait.'

'You won't find work in Harmony.' Patrick considered Dalton's frown. 'But it won't hurt to ask.'

Dalton nodded and wandered outside. He rolled over the crumbling stone wall that surrounded the church and headed into town. He walked with his back straight and with the extra rest, he was able to walk without pain. As long as he made no sudden movements, he reckoned he could appear as fit as anyone could.

A winter chill rustled damp, brown leaves down the main road, threatening to blow away the last residue of autumn and, if anyone was in town, they had the sense to stay indoors.

Amongst Harmony's dozen or so buildings there was a store, saloon and disused stable.

Dalton headed into the saloon.

The lazy buzz from the year's last flies wafted around him as he stood in the doorway. Two boys, about ten years old, sat by the door. Dotted about the room were five men who sat on their own and were silently hunched over empty coffee mugs. Milo was one of the men and along with the others he slowly lifted his head and appraised Dalton from under a lowered hat.

Dalton glanced at each man in turn, noting their bored indifference to his presence, but from the wideness of their bellies, he guessed that none of them had worked in years. Without much hope, he sauntered to the bar.

The ruddy-faced bartender provided a thin smile.

'Drink?' he asked.

'I'd like one.' Dalton leaned on the bar and smiled as the bartender reached for a whiskey bottle. 'But I can't pay.'

The bartender snorted and slipped the bottle back under the bar.

'Then you're wasting my time.' The bartender sneered and headed down the bar. 'I don't do credit.'

As Dalton turned and leaned back against the bar, Milo scraped back his chair and sauntered to the bar to stand on Dalton's right.

'I reckon you can move on,' he muttered, glaring at Dalton with an arrogant gleam in his eye, 'instead of abusin' Patrick's hospitality.'

Dalton turned to face Milo and raised his voice, ensuring that everyone in the saloon heard him.

'I aim to do just that. But I was hoping you'd tell me where I might get work until I do leave. Then I'll be minded to come in here and buy myself a drink.' Dalton raised his eyebrows. 'And one for you too.'

Milo snorted. 'In a dead-end town like Harmony, there ain't no work for *you*.'

'I ain't particular. I'll turn my hand to anything.'

Milo rubbed his chin. A slow grin emerged. 'Perhaps I do know where you'll find somethin'.'

'Go on,' Dalton murmured.

'Rock Ridge is a right boomin' town. It's fifty miles that-a-way.' Milo pointed over his shoulder. 'If you leave now, you'll get there by sundown tomorrow.'

As Milo snorted a laugh and slapped his thigh, harsh chuckles emerged from the other men in the saloon.

Dalton glanced at the grinning men, then shrugged and tipped his hat.

'Obliged for the advice. I might just do that.'

Dalton pushed from the bar and sauntered to the door. Everybody's gaze bored into the back of his neck. But he hung on to the saloon doors a moment longer than he needed to, then strode two paces down the boardwalk and leaned back against the wall, shuffling to rest on a rare non-sore spot.

The unenthusiastic sun was as high as it would get and Dalton judged that Milo was right — if he left now, he might reach Rock Ridge by sundown tomorrow. But however he looked at it, the chilly town and even chillier reception in the saloon was more hospitable than his journey would be. And if he had a choice, waiting for a warmer patch of weather would lead to a more enjoyable journey.

'You leaving, then?'

Dalton glanced to the side. A swarthy-faced man had followed him outside. Dalton shared names, learning that he was Santiago Shepperd, then lifted his foot to place the sole of his boot against the wall.

'Might be. What's it to you?'

The two boys edged into the doorway and watched Santiago with open mouths. Santiago returned a wink that raised a laugh, then matched Dalton's posture and stared into the road.

'Because if you're looking for work, you could try Chase Valdez. He might need help.'

'And where do I find him?'

'He owns the store.' Santiago pointed down the road to the second building from the saloon.

Dalton nodded as he searched Santiago's eyes for a hint of a hidden motive, but as he detected none, he tipped his hat.

'Obliged for the information.'

Santiago glanced over his shoulder at the empty saloon doorway, then whispered something to the two boys, who scurried indoors. He wandered by Dalton to stand on the opposite side to the doorway, then cupped a hand over his mouth and spoke to him from the corner of his mouth.

'Just because Milo ain't welcome in Chase's store no more, don't mean you ain't welcome too. Milo used to work for Chase. But he and Chase don't get on right now and Chase has been minding his store on his own. But now he'll need help until he's fitter.'

'What's wrong with him?'

'Sheriff Walker Dodge, that's what made him feel unwell. Yesterday Walker roared through here and gave him a beating he'll never forget.'

Dalton rubbed his ribs, wincing when his probing fingers found a sore spot.

'I'm getting to hear that lawman's name too often these days.' Dalton nodded his thanks to Santiago. 'If Chase wants my help, I owe you a drink.'

'You owe me nothing. I was just being neighbourly, friend.'

Santiago fingered his trim moustache and grinned, then paced into the saloon, leaving Dalton to head down the boardwalk and into Chase's store.

The store contained most of anything a travelling man could want. Wares clogged every available scrap of wall space and huge provisions bags flanked a snaking route to the counter.

Chase had a single forlorn wisp of hair poking from his otherwise bald pate and rolls of fat cascaded over his belt, but from the pained way that he dragged his right leg, he had something in common with Dalton.

'What do you want?' Chase asked, providing a thin smile that from the look of the deep frown lines etching his heavy jowls was a rare occurrence.

'I ain't here to buy. I've heard you're looking for help.'

Chase's smile disappeared in a moment.

'You heard wrong,' he snapped. 'I never said I wanted no help.'

'You used to employ Milo Bunch but no more. And Walker Dodge beat you.' Dalton shuffled to the counter, holding himself with a stiff back to accentuate his hurt — not too much that he would appear unfit, but enough to suggest he had injuries. 'I'm just looking to earn some money before Walker returns and I have to head out of here to avoid him beating me some more.'

Chase nodded as he watched Dalton rub his ribs.

'What did he beat you for?' he asked, his voice softer than before.

'For being on the trail.'

Chase snorted. 'Sounds a good enough reason for Walker.'

'Perhaps, so before I move on, two men who have something in common could help each other.' Dalton stretched his back, wincing with the effort.

Chase glared at Dalton, but then flexed his right leg and nodded.

'Perhaps I do need help for a week, maybe two. But it'll be back-breaking work and long hours.'

'I can work hard.'

'Then I'll pay you a dollar a week.' Chase shrugged. 'At the end of the week.'

'How much?' Dalton folded his arms. 'You expect me to suffer a whole week of back-breaking work tending for your store for just one dollar?'

'Yeah. Take it or go.'

Dalton blew out his cheeks. 'Guess you reckon I ain't got a choice.'

For the briefest of moments Chase's harsh smile appeared.

'You ain't.' Chase reached behind his counter, grabbed a broom, and held it out.

Dalton shook his head twice, then with a snort, snatched the broom from Chase's hand.

'Then I'll take it.'

3

For the remainder of the afternoon, Chase only spoke to Dalton to allocate duties to him with a few muttered grunts. And while Dalton carried out those duties, Chase shuffled around his store cussing to himself.

Whenever Dalton finished, Chase slammed his hands on his hips and stared at the result of Dalton's labours, tutting and shaking his head, then picked fault with some minor aspect of his work: He'd stacked the boxes too awkwardly; he'd stacked the boxes too straight; his sweeping didn't reach the corners of the store; his sweeping was so vigorous he'd wipe away the floor.

Dalton decided that he'd never please Chase no matter how hard he worked, so instead he devoted himself to following orders and biting his bottom lip during the inevitable admonishments.

Only three customers visited the store that afternoon and Chase dealt with them, but even then, he was curt, barely managing a flash of his weak smile when they paid their money.

He didn't offer credit.

An hour before sundown, Chase decided that no more customers were likely to arrive and that he would close the store for the day. He ordered Dalton to sweep the floor for the third time that afternoon, then hobbled through the door to his adjoining house.

As Chase left, Dalton saw him slip the few coins that he had earned today from a box under the counter and pile them in his right hand then clench his chubby fingers around them.

With the broom resting on a shoulder, Dalton sauntered to the door, keeping his footsteps light, and peered around the corner to watch Chase wander away.

Between the main house and the store there was a storeroom. Crates, boxes and bags reached to the ceiling leaving just a darkened corridor and Chase had stopped halfway along. As he watched, Chase slipped a tin box from under a pile of cloth and, from the rattling emerging from the box, Dalton guessed that a few weeks of store receipts were in there.

Dalton edged back from the door and started a steady brushing motion. He kept his back to the door as he swept, but even so the back of his neck burned giving him the sensation that Chase had returned to stand in the doorway and watch him.

Sure enough, in a pause between sweeping, he heard footsteps pace away from the doorway and back into the house.

Dalton didn't hurry his brushing and when he'd swept half the floor, he heard voices in the adjoining house. One of the voices was Chase's but the other came from a woman.

Chase had given Dalton no hint that he had a wife, but then again Chase wasn't someone with whom you engaged in banter. Dalton couldn't hear what they were saying, but from the grunts and harsh snapping, he guessed that an argument was just starting.

And from the quickness of the retorts, it was a familiar one.

Dalton leaned the brush against the wall and slipped through the doorway into the storeroom. He shuffled along the corridor between the provisions, placing his feet to the floor with deliberate care until he reached the doorway into the house, which from his ventured glance inside, he discovered was a kitchen.

He stood a moment, then risked a longer stare inside.

Standing in the middle of the kitchen was Chase and he was thrusting a finger back and forth in a woman's face while grunting a series of cusses.

The woman was younger and prettier than Dalton expected the wife of the uncompromising Chase to be. Her eyes were large and round, her lips full, a wooden bead necklace accentuated her long throat and, despite the deep scowl creasing her face, she had an exotic quality that suggested she didn't come from Harmony.

The woman slapped Chase's hand away, but Chase swung his left hand up and grabbed her wrist. She winced and slumped, trying but failing to drag her hand from Chase's grip, but with his right hand Chase slapped her cheek. The blow was sharp and echoed in the small kitchen, as did the woman's high-pitched screech.

Dalton winced, but as the woman's struggling swung her round to face the door, he edged back from the doorway. He heard another slap, then another and from the screeching, the slaps all came from Chase.

Dalton winced with each slap, but he still edged back through the storeroom. He reached the door to the store, but as yet another slap echoed around him, he sighed to himself, then backtracked. Halfway along the stacks of provisions, he knelt beside the pile of cloth. He reached underneath and grabbed the tin box, then slipped it out and opened it.

Inside were a tangle of bills and a mess of coins, perhaps twenty dollars. Dalton darted a glance towards the open door, from where the slaps had ended but a barked argument had started. The woman's responses came in another language, perhaps Spanish. Chase's retorts were nearly all cusses.

Dalton slid the money into his pocket and slipped the box back under the cloth.

As he tiptoed into the store, a huge slap from the kitchen echoed through the storeroom, followed by a crash as of the woman falling to the floor, then subdued sobbing.

But Dalton whistled under his breath, drowning out any noises coming from the kitchen, and resumed his sweeping, ensuring he did a thorough job.

Then he called back to Chase that

he'd finished, and left without waiting for permission to go.

* * *

'I'm heading to Rock Ridge,' Dalton said when he'd returned to the church.

'I'm sorry you're going.' Patrick sighed. 'But I assume that means you didn't like working for Chase Valdez.'

'Nope. That man ain't someone I'd choose to spend my time with.'

Patrick stared at Dalton with his jaw bunched in what Dalton took to be an admittance of something that a holy man couldn't voice. Then he turned to look at the cross on the church wall.

'I understand,' he whispered.

Dalton stood beside Patrick but avoided looking at the cross.

'It ain't my place to interfere with what a man and a woman do in the privacy of their own home, but I was mighty tempted to make an exception in Chase's case.'

Patrick gulped, then looked at Dalton from the corner of his eye.

'You're talking about the . . . the beatings he administers to Misty?'

'Yeah. No man can hit a woman.'

Patrick turned to face Dalton, the hint of regret in his watery eyes.

'No man can.'

'So, can't you help her, like you helped me?'

'I counsel Misty Valdez in her times of need. And you did right not to interfere, even if he was beating her. I hope that I can resolve their situation without violence.'

Dalton waited for Patrick to offer more, but as Patrick just stared at him, he smiled.

'I wish you luck.' Dalton patted Patrick's shoulder and turned to the door. 'I may see you again one day, but either way, I owe you.'

'I still hope you might stay for a while longer.'

Dalton took a step towards the door,

then stopped, but kept his gaze fixed on the door.

'You said I could leave when I wanted to.'

'I did.'

Dalton glanced over his shoulder and tipped his hat.

'Then I'm going.'

'But you could stay for dinner,' Patrick shouted. 'It's a long walk to Rock Ridge. You won't get there until tomorrow, perhaps the day after.'

A sympathetic hunger pain ripped through Dalton's guts, but he flexed his stomach and walked to the door.

'I've gone hungry before. And I've taken enough of your hospitality.'

'You haven't,' Patrick shouted after him. 'I'm here to help you with any matter that worries you — physical or spiritual.'

Dalton threw open the door. Night was creeping across the plains. A chillier wind than before whipped around his ankles and a hint of a cold rain, perhaps sleet, splashed his face.

As Dalton stood a moment, Patrick sauntered to his side and held out a hand to cup the rain, then shivered.

'I'll be walking.' Dalton shrugged his shoulders and set his collar high. 'It'll keep me warm.'

'The church will be warmer.'

'It will be.' Dalton sighed. 'But you ain't going to ask, are you?'

Patrick spread his hands wide. 'For what?'

'For me to give you something in return for your hospitality.'

'I don't need to.' Patrick held his hands wide. 'Your presence has already provided me with everything I could ask for.'

Dalton flicked his hat back on his head. 'Trying to make me feel guilty by not demanding anything won't work on me.'

'If I made you feel guilty, I apologize. I enjoyed helping you just like I enjoy helping Verna, Milo, Misty, the town orphans.'

'I saw some boys in town. I got the impression that Santiago Shepperd looks out for them.'

'He does. And that's what worries me. I'd prefer them to seek my help.' Patrick peered through the door at the annex. 'And when I've finished that extra room, maybe I can run a permanent orphanage — that is my dream.'

Dalton lifted his face to a burst of rain, trying to enjoy the coolness running across his face.

'You're a good man, Patrick.'

'You don't know me well enough to say that.' Patrick smiled. 'But go with my blessing. I will pray for you. I reckon your journey will be a long one.'

One last time Dalton tipped his hat to Patrick, then sauntered outside.

He glanced at the unfinished annex, then shrugged and headed through a gap in the church wall and down the trail. He avoided the urge to look back until he reached the point where the trail swung in to run alongside the dry gully that he had walked along to reach Harmony.

There, he stopped and looked back into town.

In the gathering gloom, Harmony was just as deserted and sleepy as it usually was.

But a single figure stood outside the church.

Dalton thought the figure was Patrick, but then realized the figure was closer than he'd originally thought and so was smaller. It was a child, possibly one of the boys from the saloon.

The child appeared to be looking at him, but then turned and scurried into Harmony.

Dalton turned and stared down the trail, imagining the fifty mile journey ahead.

He took a long pace, but then sighed and turned on the spot to look at the church.

Almost without thinking about what he was doing, he started walking towards Harmony.

'I suppose I really am hungry,' he said to himself as the rain gathered momentum and hurried him back to the church.

4

'I got no money to give you,' Dalton said, as he paced into the church doorway. 'But I reckon I can do most anything that I put my mind to. And that annex ain't building itself.'

Patrick smiled and clasped his hands together.

'If that is your wish, you should build it.'

Dalton sighed long and hard and lowered his head a moment.

'Why in tar . . . why can't you just ask me to build your annex in repayment for helping me?'

'I helped you because I wanted to help, not because I wanted you to give me something in return.' Patrick considered Dalton's scowl, then shrugged and lowered his voice. 'But if helping to finish the annex will please you, do that.'

‘That wasn’t too difficult,’ Dalton muttered, then walked outside with Patrick following him.

The rain had set in to a steady drizzle as Patrick raised a foot on the heap of rocks.

‘How much would you like to do?’

Dalton glanced at the complete annex to his side.

‘I don’t reckon I can build a roof that won’t leak, but I can build the walls.’

Patrick nodded his thanks and returned to the church, leaving Dalton to seek shelter behind the highest length of wall and pick appropriate rocks for the next layer. For an hour he worked before the enticing smell of Verna’s cooking emerging from the church dragged him inside.

Verna had cooked another heap of stew and along with Patrick and Milo, Dalton tucked into two helpings and even half-jokingly asked if he could lick the pot clean.

Verna refused his offer with a sharp tap on the wrist from her spoon, which drew the first laugh Dalton had heard from Patrick. So Dalton baited Verna some more by licking his plate clean.

Throughout, Patrick watched Dalton with what Dalton took to be benign approval at his appetite and, he hoped, gratitude for his help.

With dinner eaten, Verna washed the plates and pot, then headed into the main church for Patrick to lead her in prayers. Milo wandered off again, presumably to the saloon.

Dalton stood in the doorway and watched. Again Patrick neither invited him to join him nor looked at him. And if Patrick was encouraging Dalton to pray by trying to make him feel guilty, Dalton reckoned he could withstand the pressure.

Just as Patrick was finishing a hymn, insistent knocking thundered on the main door, echoing through the church and causing Verna to start.

Patrick ordered Verna to hide in Dalton's room, which she did with practised speed. Patrick glanced at

Dalton, conveying with a glance that this could be Sheriff Walker Dodge and that he should hide. But Dalton shook his head and with a sigh and a roll of his shoulders, Patrick strode to the door.

Dalton pushed from the doorway and strode into the aisle to stand five paces behind Patrick.

With a last glance at Dalton, Patrick threw the door open, but before he could speak, Chase Valdez pushed him aside and stood in the doorway with his squat legs set wide and his flabby jowls shaking with indignation.

'You thieving varmint,' he roared, glaring at Dalton and aiming a trembling finger at him.

'It's nice to see you too,' Dalton said. He forced a wide smile and walked down the aisle to join Patrick. 'Come on in and join the praying.'

'I ain't setting foot in this place.'

'You're always welcome to enter,' Patrick said, holding his arms wide.

'I ain't doing that.' Chase leaned into

the church to stab a firm finger at Dalton's chest, but still kept his feet planted on the church steps. 'That good-for-nothing varmint stole from me.'

Dalton snorted. 'The only person looking to steal was you. I wasn't working for a whole week for one dollar.'

Chase slammed his hands on his hips. 'So you stole fifty dollars from me instead.'

Dalton glanced away, muttering under his breath, but Patrick paced before him and faced Chase.

'I've heard many things about you, Chase, but that accusation against a man who only wanted to help you doesn't become you.'

'That ain't no accusation. Dalton sneaked into my house and stole my money.'

'You see him do it?'

'No, but — '

'Just because Walker Dodge beat you it doesn't mean you have the right to take out your anger on strangers.' Patrick lowered his voice. 'Or on people you know.'

Chase's eyes narrowed. 'You got something to say to me, just say it.'

Patrick lowered his head a moment, then patted Dalton's shoulder.

'I'll just say this, Walker beat Dalton too and his response was to do something positive like helping me to build the annex outside.'

Chase threw back his head and grunted a hollow laugh.

'Then watch your valuables. The only person he helps is himself.'

'I didn't steal your money,' Dalton snapped. 'I just prefer to work for nothing here than work for next-to-nothing for a no-good, lousy — '

'Dalton,' Patrick said, 'you are in a house of God and whatever the provocation, you do not swear.'

'I'm sorry. But I didn't steal Chase's money.' Dalton took a half-pace forward and sneered at Chase. 'I just wouldn't take money from the likes of you. The money would have touched your dirty hands.'

Chase flexed his fists, but then only shook one in Dalton's face.

'I'll be watching you, Dalton. I'll get that money back before your thieving hands get a chance to spend it.'

Chase glared at Dalton and Patrick in turn, then turned and waddled into the night, favouring his right leg.

'Thanks for speaking up for me.' Dalton turned to Patrick. 'But there was no need.'

'Just didn't want rumours to start. Once people start thinking a stranger is bad, people can't be convinced that he's decent.'

'Obliged.' Dalton grabbed the door to close it, but as Verna slipped back into the church and knelt before the altar, he took a pace outside instead.

'Where are you going?' Patrick asked.

'Into town.' Dalton rolled his shoulders and pulled his hat low to shelter his face from the rain. 'Don't worry. I ain't going after Chase, but as I'll be here a while, I reckon you were right. I have to stop those rumours before they start.'

Dalton patted Patrick's shoulder and sauntered outside. He waited until Patrick closed the door behind him, then peered into town.

Fifty yards ahead was Chase's bulky form, but he'd set a shoulder down and was walking in a purposeful manner that didn't suggest he'd hear anyone walking behind him.

Even so, Dalton kept well back until Chase reached town and when Chase hobbled onto the boardwalk, he edged to the side of the road and hid while Chase barged into his store. Then he resumed his walk through town and into the saloon, but he gave the store a wide margin.

Inside the saloon, the same customers as this morning were hunched over glasses, each with a puddle of whiskey in the bottom. Dalton nodded to Santiago, receiving a nod, and to Milo, receiving a harsh glare.

The bartender looked up, a smile on his lips, but then frowned on seeing that the newcomer was just Dalton.

'What do you want this time?' he grunted.

'Nothing,' Dalton said, smiling broadly. 'I still can't pay for a drink.'

Milo snorted and muttered to himself.

'Reckoned as you'd have money now,' the bartender said, folding his arms.

'I worked for Chase today but he didn't pay me.'

'That ain't what I mean.' For long moments the bartender glared at Dalton, but as Dalton returned the glare, he grabbed a cloth and wiped it across the bar. 'Chase reckons you stole fifty dollars from him.'

'He can reckon all he likes.' Dalton sauntered across the saloon. He leaned back against the bar and looked around the room, ending his appraisal at Milo. 'But that man's a mean varmint, a woman beater, and a liar.'

Muffled agreements drifted around the saloon, but Milo scraped back a chair and stalked to the bar to stand to Dalton's side.

'We know about the first two,' he said. 'But I ain't sure about the last.'

'You reckon I got it wrong?'

'Nope. I reckon there's only one liar here.' Milo licked his lips and raised on his heels so that he shared Dalton's eye-line. 'And that's you.'

Dalton glanced at Santiago, who shrugged, then returned his gaze to Milo.

'And am I lying when I say the only person abusing Patrick's hospitality is you?'

Milo grunted and hurled a fist at Dalton's face, but Dalton deflected the blow with his left forearm and clipped Milo's chin with his right fist.

The blow hit with little force, but Milo's head still rocked back.

Milo staggered back a step, then righted himself and rolled his shoulders. He advanced a long pace and threw a fist at Dalton's jaw, but Dalton swayed from it and smashed a blow to Milo's cheek that sent him sprawling to the floor.

Milo rolled to his feet and stormed back in, flailing his fists, but Dalton just raised his arms and took the blows, waiting for an opening. When it came, he thundered a blow to Milo's jaw that lifted his feet from the ground before he hit the floor on his back and slid five feet.

Milo lay a moment, rubbing his jaw, then tottered to his feet and stood hunched. Dalton didn't wait until he regained his senses and advanced on him, instead he grabbed his jacket, turned him round, and ran him through the doorway.

He watched the swing-doors creak to a halt, and when Milo didn't return, he batted his hands together and returned to the bar.

'Anyone else want to call me a liar?' he said, his voice calm.

Several men glared at him, but with a

ripple of shrugs, everyone then returned to their drinks.

'I'll take that for a no, but just so everyone's clear I'm passing through on my way to Rock Ridge. I'm helping Patrick Williams build his annex. It'll take a week and when I've finished, I'll move on.' Dalton took a last glance around the bar. 'I'm an honest man and I ain't looking for trouble, but if anyone calls me a liar, I'll deal with them.'

The bartender glanced away. But Santiago was grinning at him and, with a dart of his index finger, tipped his hat.

Dalton returned a nod, then strode outside.

He expected Milo to be lying in wait on the boardwalk, so he waited a moment, letting his eyes accustom to the gloom. From under a lowered hat, he surveyed each shadow coating the buildings opposite, but he detected no movements, so he shrugged and headed down the boardwalk towards the church.

'That's far enough,' a voice muttered

from the alley beside the saloon.

From the corner of his eye, Dalton glanced to the side. In the alley, he saw the glint of gun-metal and behind that, the fevered grin and bright eyes of Milo.

'Ain't no need for that,' he said. He raised his hands to shoulder level showing that he didn't wear a gunbelt, then opened his jacket to show he didn't wear a shoulder strap. 'I ain't packing a gun.'

'You ain't. But you have the look of someone who normally does.'

'Then you shouldn't have returned with a gun and escalated this. As far as I was concerned, we'd closed our argument.'

'It ain't closed.' Milo gestured, causing the gunmetal shine to disappear and when he spoke again his voice was lower and came from deeper into the alley. 'And unless you get yourself a gun, stay out of town.'

Dalton stood a moment, straining to hear whether Milo had left the alley, and on hearing nothing but the light patter of rain on his hat, he took a long pace into the alley.

For long moments Dalton stared into the dark until he could see well enough to walk without risking that he would crash into something, then stalked down the alley.

When Dalton reached the other end and peered around the corner in all directions, Milo had already melted into the shadows.

Dalton shrugged and slipped back down the alley and headed to the church.

The road was deserted. But Dalton felt as if Milo's gaze was boring into his back.

Even so, Dalton didn't hurry.

5

At sun-up, Dalton started work on the first wall of Patrick's annex.

He judged that if he devoted himself to the work, he'd complete it in less than the week he'd originally agreed with Patrick, perhaps even within five days.

Why Patrick had spent so long failing to make progress with his building, Dalton didn't like to enquire, so instead he worked steadily, only pausing to eat and to acknowledge Patrick and Verna when they left for their daily rounds. If Milo had returned to the church, he didn't see him and he didn't detect any interest in his lack of presence from Verna.

Mid-morning, Santiago Shepperd sauntered from town. The two boys sat on the wall and watched him stand beside Dalton and look his building work up and down with an appraising eye.

'You're doing a mighty fine job here,' he said.

'I am,' Dalton replied, standing back from the wall to stretch his back.

'Patrick paying you as much as Chase?'

'Less.'

Santiago chuckled. 'That's hard to imagine.'

'It is, but I enjoy his company more.'

Santiago nodded. 'I can see that. But enjoyment won't feed a man once he leaves Harmony.'

'Yeah.' Dalton considered Chase, then grabbed his next rock. 'And how do you earn enough to feed yourself?'

Santiago licked his lips, then placed his head over the part of the wall where Dalton was about to lay the next rock.

'I buy,' he whispered. 'I sell.'

'You're Chase's competitor?'

'Nope.' Santiago rubbed his chin and stood tall. 'You won't find what I buy and sell in Chase's store.'

'Then I'll remember you if I need something I can't buy from Chase.' Dalton tossed the rock from hand to hand. 'But don't get your hopes up. I have no money.'

'But Milo's boasting that he'll kill you for stealing from Chase.'

'He's all talk. That man ain't even got the nerve to return here to sleep.'

Dalton moved to place the rock on the wall again, but Santiago sat on the wall, forcing Dalton to stand to the side.

'Milo's as yellow-bellied as they come, but a scared man with a gun is more dangerous than a brave man without one.'

'If things are that dangerous, I'll get a gun.'

'Ain't many in Harmony who pack guns and the nearest gunsmith is in Rock Ridge.' Santiago slipped a cheroot from his pocket and slammed it into the corner of his mouth, unlit. 'But I can obtain anything a man wants — provided he can pay.'

'Then it's a pity I don't want anything. And it's a pity I can't pay.'

Santiago rolled the cheroot to the other corner of his mouth and ran a finger along his thin moustache.

'Like you say, it's a pity.'

'I can see you're still hoping I'm a source of business, but as I don't reckon Milo's got the guts to kill me, I ain't interested.'

'Then what about Walker Dodge?'

'I'll leave before he returns.'

'And Chase?'

'Chase wouldn't take on anyone who ain't a woman.'

'Don't be so sure about him.' Santiago removed his cheroot and considered it. 'He has plenty of reasons to kill a thief.'

'Then I'm glad I ain't a thief,' Dalton snapped and pushed Santiago from his wall. 'Now leave me. I got work to do, even if you ain't.'

'I have work to do all the time, Dalton.'

Santiago leaned back against the

church wall, slipped the cheroot back into his mouth, and grinned around it.

Dalton lifted his rock to place it on the wall, but then dropped it to the ground at his feet and folded his arms.

'I got the feeling you're trying to tell me something.' Dalton raised his hands and stared at the palms, then bunched them into fists a moment before relaxing and dropping them to his sides. 'But I'd be obliged if you'd just spell it out. I ain't got the time to waste in idle musing.'

'I ain't accusing you of anything. But I was musing idly about Chase.' Santiago chuckled. 'There are so many tales about him that it's hard to know what is true and what is just saloon talk. A stranger might look at Chase and reckon he's a dour, fat nobody with a fine woman that he doesn't deserve as a wife.'

Dalton raised a foot on his rock pile and leaned on his knee.

'That pretty much sums up what I saw.'

'But if you listen to the saloon talk, you'd hear that Misty came from a rich family as repayment of an old debt. You'd hear that she came to Chase wearing a fabulous ruby necklace that is worth more than the whole of Harmony. And you'd hear that Chase has kept the necklace for himself and forced Misty to wear a wooden bead necklace instead.'

Dalton snorted. 'So Misty owned a fabulous necklace, but nobody has seen it?'

'That is what you might believe, if you were to believe the saloon talk.'

'And who provides that saloon talk?'

'Many people. Some even claim to have seen the necklace.' Santiago glanced around, then leaned to Dalton. 'Milo Bunch for one. Last month when he was lurking down by the gully in the dead of night, he saw Misty dancing in the moonlight. That alone should have entranced him, but the rubies around her neck stole every last shred of common sense he had left.'

‘A lowlife like Milo might claim many things just so other people would reckon he had some worth.’ Dalton rubbed his chin. ‘So how sure is he of what he saw?’

‘Sure enough to tell everyone when he got drunk. Sure enough for Chase to run him out of his store. Sure enough to tell Walker Dodge to gain some respite from that man’s incessant tormenting. And maybe sure enough to kill you because he reckons a thief will steal the necklace before he does.’

Dalton lifted his foot from the rock pile, grabbed a rock, then juggled it from hand to hand.

‘And do you believe it’s more than a tale?’

‘I believe Walker is convinced it exists, so much so that he nearly beat Chase to death when he wouldn’t tell him where it is and will do so again when he returns. So much so that just about the only thing that’s keeping Milo alive is Walker’s belief that he’s the best man to find it.’

'A mighty interesting story.' Dalton slammed the rock on the top of the wall. 'But I ain't staying here long enough to find out if it's true. I'm just building this annex, then heading on to Rock Ridge.'

Dalton knelt beside the pile of rocks and sorted through them for a suitable rock to fill the next gap in the wall. He kept his head downturned for far longer then he needed to and when he rose, he checked the wall on the opposite side of the annex to Santiago.

Santiago watched Dalton as he made a big show of ignoring him, then pushed from the wall and wandered around the annex.

'Just be careful, Dalton,' he whispered. 'Misty is also more dangerous than she appears.'

Santiago collected the boys, then sauntered into Harmony.

Dalton firmed his jaw and returned to working at a steady pace, but after laying another five rocks, he glanced to the side to see that Santiago had disappeared back into town.

Dalton let a smile crease the corners of his mouth.

* * *

'Get away!' Chase muttered, bunching his fists.

Dalton raised his hands, palms outstretched, as he strode into the store.

'You got me wrong. I didn't steal from you. I heard you *arguing* with Misty, and as it ain't my place to get involved with what happens between a man and a woman in their own home, I just swept out the store and left. Don't know what I can say to make you believe that.'

'Then don't bother trying.' Chase pointed a chubby finger at Dalton. 'Sheriff Walker Dodge can deal with you.'

Dalton rubbed his ribs. 'Walker beat you just like he beat me.'

'Yeah, but perhaps if he has a thief to

beat, he won't bother with me.' Chase hobbled out from behind the counter and grabbed Dalton's arm. 'Now get out and stay away from my money.'

Dalton set his feet wide and resisted Chase's attempt to drag him to the door.

'Chase, I don't want Walker after me. I just want to prove to you that I'm an honest man.'

Chase tugged Dalton's arm again, but finding no give, he released his grip and squared his jowled jaw.

'Giving me back my money will prove that.'

'I can't do that. But I can work for you until you're fitter. And you do need help now that Milo ain't here no more.' Dalton shook a fist and raised his eyebrows. 'And I've been hearing rumours about that man and how he crossed you. And if he crosses you again, I'll just have to knock him down like I did last night.'

A momentary smile invaded Chase's flabby features.

'You beat Milo?'

'Sure did.'

For long moments Chase glared at Dalton, but as Dalton continued to stare at him, Chase nodded.

'Perhaps I was harsh on you,' he murmured.

'You were.'

Chase waggled a finger at Dalton. 'But if I let you work here again, I'll watch your every movement.'

'I know. But I also want to leave Harmony with some real money in my pocket. What you offered me yesterday ain't enough to make it worth my while. So I'll only work if you pay me a dollar a day and you pay me at the end of each day.'

Chase slammed his hands on his hips.

'You rob me in the dark and now you're robbing me in the daylight.'

'I just want to help myself as much as help you.' Dalton held his hands wide. 'And if I'd stolen your fifty dollars, do you think I'd be in Rock Ridge by now or do you think I'd be festering away here?'

'Perhaps not,' Chase murmured.

'As soon as I have enough money to let me eat for a week or two in Rock Ridge, I'm leaving. Until then, you're the only person offering work.'

'Don't care about that. If you want those kind of wages, it ain't worth my while.'

'Then put it this way, either you employ me or you employ someone else. And the only person who's interested in working for you is Milo Bunch.' Dalton shrugged. 'And I'm sure you don't want him in your store.'

Chase winced and stared at the floor a moment.

'All right,' he murmured. 'I'll pay fifty cents a day.'

'Obliged.'

Chase hobbled from the counter, but he stopped in the doorway to the storeroom and glanced over his shoulder.

'But remember this, Dalton. No

matter what Santiago Shepperd has told you, Misty has never owned no ruby necklace.' Chase grinned as Dalton was unable to stop himself from wincing. 'So, do you still want to work for me?'

6

Chase was true to his promised untrusting attitude towards Dalton.

He banned Dalton from straying into his storeroom. Any money his customers paid disappeared into his inside jacket pocket instantly and afterwards he glared at Dalton and patted his pocket as if to check that Dalton hadn't somehow spirited the money away.

The heavy sarcasm didn't concern Dalton, but what did irritate him was that Chase did no work and instead devoted his time to watching Dalton's every movement.

Dalton had decided Chase would have claimed that the necklace didn't exist whether it did or not, but with Chase giving him no leeway, he couldn't even start his search for it.

So he decided not to risk the rewards from two weeks' work by acting on

Santiago's dubious saloon talk and for the rest of the day made no effort to look for hiding places. Even during the occasional times when Chase left him alone, he still passed up the opportunity to search the store.

That night, as soon as Chase had paid him for his day's work, he headed outside. On the boardwalk he stood a moment, listening to Chase raising his voice to Misty inside, but he was searching for any movements in town. From the corner of his eye, he reckoned he saw someone, perhaps Milo, scurry down an alley that was between him and the church.

Dalton shrugged and headed down the road in the opposite direction.

Once out of town, he doubled back around the outskirts of town, on the opposite side, until he reached the church.

On this longer journey he saw nobody.

He agreed with Patrick that as he was now working for Chase, the work on the annex would take longer than he expected. But Patrick was delighted that Dalton had had the courage to seek work with a man that had accused him of being a thief.

After a short meal, Dalton used the last hour of daylight to add another row of stone to the annex. It was only when Verna emerged after praying with Patrick and headed into the completed annex that Dalton stood, stretched his back, and sauntered into the church.

Patrick was praying alone but he looked up when Dalton entered.

'You've worked hard today, Dalton.'

Despite himself, Dalton puffed his chest.

'I have.' He patted his pocket. 'And I also have me some wages. It ain't much, but it's the first money I've seen since Walker Dodge bushwhacked me and if there's a thief around, I could do with hiding it.'

'There are no hiding places in the church. You should just keep it on you.' Patrick watched Dalton nod, then gestured to a spot before the altar. 'I would welcome you joining me.'

'Sorry. I ain't the praying type.' Dalton sighed. 'And quit hoping you'll kindle some faith in me and we'll get on fine for the next two weeks. Save your efforts for your followers.'

Patrick's eyes watered before he blinked the moisture away.

'I have no followers.'

'You have Verna and . . . ' Dalton coughed. 'And Milo.'

'They like the shelter and wish to please me, so Verna prays.' Patrick patted his chest. 'I am more interested in what is in a man's heart. A righteous man continuing to be righteous is of little consequence, but when a sinner repents, that will fill me with joy.'

'And you reckon I'm a sinner?'

'I can't judge that, only you can know what is in your heart.'

'Worry about yourself, not me. In another two weeks, I'll be gone, but you'll still be here and you'll have to deal with all the troubles in Harmony.'

Patrick's eyes flickered with the hint of something, perhaps doubt, before he blinked it away.

'I will.'

'You don't sound so sure of yourself.' Dalton sat on the front pew and rested his hands on his knees. 'Is there anything you'd like to tell me?'

Patrick hung his head a moment, then set his earnest gaze on Dalton.

'Two days ago I was ready to seek a . . . a different path, but your arrival convinced me to continue with my chosen path. And now, I believe the choices you make mean more to me than anyone else's choices — perhaps even whether I was right to keep my faith.'

Dalton stood, shaking his head. 'You've put your faith in the wrong man.'

'I don't think so.'

Dalton bid his goodnights then went to his room and rolled under his blanket.

But he could hear Patrick praying, and even when he stopped, his mumbling seemed to invade the whole church. Dalton pressed his hands to his ears, pulled the blanket over his head, but nothing drowned Patrick's low susurration, and so Dalton jumped to his feet, grabbed his blanket and left his room.

As he headed outside, he avoided catching Patrick's eye. An overcast sky had driven away the coldness that had descended on Harmony for the last few days and with this extra warmth, he found a comfortable spot in the corner of the annex. Within minutes, he was asleep.

The next day, and for the following five days, he adopted a standard pattern to his day.

He rose at sun-up, worked for an hour on the annex, then headed to the store. He worked diligently all day, ignoring Chase's chides and muttering, then at the end of the day, returned to the church, but always by a different route that avoided any chance of Milo waylaying him.

He didn't see Milo at all.

For an hour he worked on the annex, ate his dinner, then worked for another hour before retiring to his blanket to sleep in the corner of the annex.

In his periodic restful moments he shared stilted conversation with Patrick. Dalton could see that Patrick wanted to turn the conversation to matters of faith and the choices facing him, but Dalton redirected his attempts.

A week after Dalton had arrived in Harmony, Chase's poor mood hadn't improved but his injuries were and he started to mutter more and more that he'd only need Dalton for another three or four days.

As Patrick also suggested that Walker Dodge would return soon, perhaps within the next day or so, Dalton resolved to leave town as soon as he could. So he lit a fire to give him sufficient light to work long into the night on the annex.

So some four hours after sundown, he saw a figure scurry out of town and towards the church. The figure was slight. But in the poor light Dalton couldn't be sure that it wasn't Milo so he rolled his trowel into the back of his hand and feigned studious interest in the latest rock he'd placed on the wall.

But as the figure approached, he realized it was too small to be Milo and when it had edged through the collapsed length of church wall, twenty yards away, he realized it was Misty.

He smiled and tipped his hat as she paced to the door, but she wrapped her shawl more tightly around her shoulders and kept her gaze on the church door until she could slip inside.

Dalton edged to the door and listened, but aside from low voices, which were probably Patrick and Misty praying, he heard no distinct words. He shrugged and returned to his building.

An hour later, when Dalton retired for the night, she still hadn't emerged from the church.

7

'I need a bag of corn.'

Dalton was stacking boxes in the corner of the store when he heard Misty's request, but he kept his gaze set forward and avoided looking at her.

'Misty,' Chase snapped, 'you know those bags are still too heavy for me.'

'I know,' Misty said, edging into the store, 'but I need corn or you won't eat tonight.'

Chase muttered to himself, but Dalton coughed and turned.

'I'll help,' he said.

Chase grunted his disapproval of this offer, but Dalton ignored him and weaved past Chase to a stack of corn bags. With Chase's gaze boring into his back, Dalton grabbed a sack, hoisted it on his right shoulder, and carried it past Chase and out of the store.

Misty and Chase shared low words

then they both followed two paces behind, but just as Chase entered the kitchen a customer wandered into the store and called to Chase.

Chase edged back and forth, then waddled back into the store to deal with him.

'Thank you,' Misty said as Dalton thudded the bag on to the kitchen table.

Dalton tipped his hat. 'And don't feed Chase all that corn in one go, or he'll get as fat as a pig.'

A short titter escaped Misty's lips before she clamped a hand over her mouth, then darted her gaze away from Dalton as she fingered the wooden beads at her neck.

Dalton stood a moment, smiling.

'Did your praying with — '

Misty flared her eyes and waved her arms, signifying that Dalton should stop this question and with that command, Dalton hung his head, searching for something else to say. But as he couldn't find anything, he tipped his hat again and returned to the store.

Chase glared at him from the corner of his eye, but said nothing as he dealt with his customer, so Dalton stood behind the counter and when the customer had left, Chase made no effort to talk to him.

That evening, when Chase closed the shop, Dalton volunteered for the sweeping duties.

Although Chase patted his pocket and the bulge of today's receipts, he left him alone at the end of the day for the first time since he'd restarted working here.

Within a minute, Dalton heard raised voices in the kitchen. He swept the broom back and forth briskly to drown out the words, but when this failed he laid the broom on the counter and edged through the doorway. With a hand to his ear, he stood midway between the store and the kitchen.

'What did you say to him?' Chase snapped.

'Who?' Misty said.

'Dalton. Who else do you see?'

'Nothing.'

'You were laughing.'

'He just said something funny.'

'What?'

Dalton edged into the doorway and peered around the door.

Chase was facing away from Dalton with his hands set on his wide hips and standing before Misty, but Misty's gaze was only on Chase.

'I can't remember,' she whispered.

Chase raised a fist. 'Then think.'

Misty cringed back a pace. 'He just said your corn is mighty fine.'

'And that's funny?' Chase roared, lifting his fist high. 'Why?'

Misty winced and shrugged away from a blow that didn't come. Still she backed to the wall.

'I can't remember why. It just was at the time.'

'Then think some more.' Chase rolled his shoulder. 'And then you can make me laugh.'

'It *was* funny,' Dalton said, stepping

into the doorway. 'Just you ain't got a sense of humour.'

Chase swirled round with his fists raised.

'What you doing back here?'

'Don't want you to think that I interfere between what a man and a woman do in the privacy of their own home.' Dalton held his hands wide and put on his widest grin. 'But I'm just telling you what happened earlier.'

'I never asked you for no opinion.'

'You didn't. But I try to be right neighbourly whenever I can.'

Chase glared back at Dalton, then shrugged and lowered his fists.

'Yeah, well that don't mean you can steal my money.'

Dalton winced. 'You've watched me and I've done nothing to make you think I'm a thief.'

'You ain't thieving no more because I *am* watching you.'

'That's wrong. But I'll be gone soon and I don't want you thinking that I robbed you.'

Chase waddled across the kitchen to stand before Dalton.

'Then answer me this — if you didn't take my money, who did?'

Dalton rubbed his chin. 'I don't rightly know, but I wouldn't look no further than your former worker, who seems mighty keen on causing trouble. And I reckon you know he did it too.'

'Milo is a good-for-nothing varmint. But he wouldn't steal.' Chase snorted. 'He ain't nowhere near clever enough for that.'

'Listen to Dalton,' Misty said. 'Milo was always — '

'Be quiet, woman,' Chase shouted, swirling round to glare at Misty. 'I never asked your opinion either.'

Misty hung her head and backed along the wall to stand in the corner. Her shoulders drooped and Dalton reckoned he saw a solitary tear fall to the floor. But when Chase turned back, Dalton tipped his hat.

'If you ain't interested in my opinion,' he said, 'I'll bid you goodnight. If I get the chance to shake the truth out of Milo before I go, I'll let you know what he says.'

For long moments Chase glared at Dalton. Then his shoulders slumped and he nodded.

'I'd be obliged if you'd do that. That man always was no good.'

Dalton paced from the kitchen, through the storeroom, and into the store. He grabbed the broom, but then threw it on the counter and wandered outside. On the boardwalk, he listened to the voices in the kitchen, but now they were low and Dalton hoped they were also contented.

From above he heard a clatter and a shadow ripped across the boardwalk, but even as he flinched away a solid blow landed on his back, flattening him to the ground.

Dalton just had time to realize that someone had jumped on his back from the roof, before his assailant rolled from him and dragged him to his feet and back to the wall.

Still disorientated, Dalton squirmed, aiming to free himself, but then saw that his assailant was Milo. Dalton slumped and let Milo throw him back against the wall.

'I told you to stay out of town,' Milo muttered.

Dalton shrugged his jacket straight and stood tall.

'I don't take orders from the likes of you.'

Milo rolled his shoulders, then ripped his gun from its holster and aimed it at Dalton's chest.

'You will if you want to live.'

Dalton kept his gaze on Milo's eyes. 'You're all talk, Milo. You ain't got the guts to take me on for real. I've worked here for a week and you just ain't been around. Seems as if you've been avoiding me.'

Milo thrust his gun out, but the hand shook with a slight tremor.

'I have been around and I've watched you every time you came into town and every time you left. I could have killed you any time I wanted to.'

'I ain't seen you.'

'Then that's your problem.' Milo gestured to the store door. 'So why was Misty defendin' you in there? Are you and her gettin' close? Because Chase won't like that.'

'How did you hear that?'

Milo grinned. 'As I say, I've been watchin' you. All that's keepin' you alive is that I'm waitin' for you to do more thievin'. And when you do — '

'I ain't no thief.'

Milo snorted and backed from Dalton to pace off the boardwalk, then thrust his gun in its holster.

'Then if you're no thief, that was your only warnin'. The next time, you'll be dead before you realize you've made a mistake.'

Milo hitched his gunbelt a mite higher, then turned and swaggered down the road.

Dalton watched him until he headed into the saloon, then strode down the road in the opposite direction.

Leaning against the stable at the end of the road was Santiago, a wide grin on his face and his gaze roving between the saloon and Dalton.

Dalton tipped his hat, but Santiago pushed from the wall to stand before him.

'Remember, Dalton,' he said. 'I can get anything a man wants.'

'I've remembered,' Dalton grunted.

'So, do you want that gun now?'

Dalton veered to the side to walk by Santiago, but two paces past him he stopped and turned.

'I ain't escalating my argument with Milo. I'm just fulfilling my obligations until I can head to Rock Ridge.'

'Of course you are, Dalton.' Santiago rubbed a finger along his moustache and lowered his voice. 'Of course you are.'

* * *

After dinner, Dalton again worked on the annex.

Around an hour after the half-moon had set, as last night, Misty emerged from Harmony and trotted towards the church.

Again, Dalton tipped his hat as she approached the church door, but this time she stopped and joined him.

'Thank you for speaking up for me earlier,' she said. She smiled, but then thinned her full lips with a harsh frown. 'Don't do it again.'

'I'm sorry. I shouldn't have interfered in no dispute between a man and woman in the privacy of their own home, but when I heard raised voices, and my name was uttered, I had to do something.'

'You're a good man.' Misty rubbed her arm and turned towards the church. 'But please don't make my life more difficult.'

'Did he beat you?'

Misty rocked back and forth on her heels, then turned back to Dalton.

'He always beats me. If you hadn't have interfered, he would have hit me the once or twice, but you made his anger fester for longer, and when it broke, he really put some effort into it.'

'I'm sorry.' Dalton hung his head. 'I didn't know.'

'You did what you thought was best.' Misty nodded and turned to the church. 'And I need to pray now.'

'Does Chase know you come here?' he shouted after her.

'No,' she said with a hand on the door.

'Won't he beat you some more if he finds out you've gone?'

'He won't.' She snorted a short, humourless chuckle, then pushed the door open. 'I sneaked out of my bedroom window. And my bedroom is one place he never goes. Good night, Dalton.'

8

In the morning, Chase was still gruff with Dalton, but no more or less than before.

Whether he was still brooding over Dalton's intervention into his argument with Misty or not, Dalton didn't know. But he made no effort to discover the truth as he followed Chase's barked orders.

Early in the afternoon, Misty shuffled into the store. She spoke to neither Chase nor Dalton as she located a small bag of salt then headed back into the house, but as she passed Dalton, she glanced at him and flashed him the briefest of smiles.

Dalton smiled back, but on seeing Chase looking at him, he firmed his jaw and leaned over the counter.

Chase muttered oaths to himself while slapping his fist against his thigh, then swirled round on the spot and strode into the house. As his firm footfalls paced into the kitchen, Dalton fixed his gaze on the front door.

'Why were you smiling at Dalton?' Chase roared, his voice loud enough to rip through the storeroom.

Misty murmured something, but Dalton couldn't hear the words.

'And that's a reason?' Chase grunted an oath as Misty sobbed. 'I said, is that a reason?'

Dalton stood a moment, wincing, then pushed from the counter. He paced into the storeroom, down the corridor between the provisions, and stopped outside the kitchen to stare through the doorway.

Inside, Chase stood hunched with his hands on his hips.

'Seems to me,' Chase said, glaring at Misty, 'that you get too many ideas about any man I employ.'

Misty closed her eyes a moment. 'I'm mighty glad that you removed Milo. You know that.'

‘Is that because you like Dalton more?’

‘Chase,’ Misty said, ‘please don’t say things like that.’

Chase snorted and slapped Misty’s cheek, forcing Misty to stumble to her knees, her hands raised to ward off the next blow.

In the doorway, Dalton rocked back and forth on his heels, his hands opening and closing, but then backed into the storeroom and into the store. Even there, he heard two more slaps, then a firmer blow and a screech.

Within the kitchen, silence then reigned so that Dalton could only hear himself grind his teeth.

Then Chase paced back into the store. He rolled his shoulders and glared at Dalton.

‘Anything wrong, Dalton?’ he grunted.

Dalton grabbed a cloth and swept it across the counter.

‘Like I said yesterday,’ he said, ‘it ain’t my place to speak up about what goes on between a man and a woman in the privacy of their own home.'

Chase stalked round to stand on the other side of the counter facing Dalton and slammed a clammy hand on Dalton's hand, halting his wiping.

'But if you were to speak up, what would you say?'

Dalton kept his gaze downcast and chewed on his bottom lip.

'I might just wonder,' he whispered, 'why a man has to hurt a woman who is barely half his size.'

'You might wonder that, might you?' Chase ripped the cloth from Dalton's grasp and hurled it away. 'Well, I reckon you've done too much wondering for my liking. I reckon you can leave work now.'

Dalton raised his gaze, but forced a smile to emerge.

'You still need me. You ain't hobbling, but you have trouble lifting anything heavy.'

'I reckon I'm all fixed now.' Chase reached into his pocket and extracted a dollar bill. 'Here's your payment for the rest of today and tomorrow. Now, you got no reason to stay.'

Dalton glared at Chase a moment, then shrugged and pocketed the bill. He tipped his hat and sauntered out from behind the counter, but at Chase's side he stopped and glanced at him from the corner of his eye.

'Just so you know — once I've finished my business in Rock Ridge, I'll head back this way.' Dalton patted Chase's shoulder with an insistent rhythm. 'It might be a year, or then again it might be two. But when I do, I'll look in on you.'

'Ain't no need.' Chase batted Dalton's hand away. 'I ain't enjoyed your company.'

'But I reckon I will. Because then I can see whether Misty has any bruises on her. And if I find a single mark, I'll return all the blows you've rained down on her ten-fold.' Dalton tipped back his hat and leaned forward to thrust his face inches from Chase's face. 'And I won't stop until you're just a disgusting stain on your well-swept floor.'

Dalton grabbed Chase's collar and pulled him up tight.

Chase glared down at Dalton's hand, a bead of sweat breaking out on his brow.

'You can't threaten me.'

'I ain't. I'm just telling you I'll be looking in on you and Misty.' Dalton pulled Chase up tight to his nose and widened his eyes. 'Understand?'

For a long moment Chase glared back, but then glanced away.

'Yeah.'

Dalton snorted and threw Chase back against the counter, but Chase rebounded and came up with a defiant glare in his eyes and his hands set on his hips.

Dalton snorted and swung back his fist. He thundered a blow into Chase's flabby guts that knocked him back against the counter. And as Chase floundered, he followed through with an uppercut to the chin that wheeled him over the counter to clatter in a heap on the other side.

'And that was just something to remember the next time you fancy raising your fist to a woman,' Dalton muttered, batting his hands together.

As Chase whined and clutched his guts, Dalton pulled his hat low and stalked to the door and outside.

For once, as he returned to the church, he didn't look out for Milo.

* * *

Even without the irritation of his confrontation with Chase, Dalton would have tried to complete the wall that day. But with excess energy coursing through his muscles, he slammed rocks on the wall with a steady rhythm for the rest of the day and well into evening.

He didn't even pause to talk with Santiago when he emerged from town to offer additional less-than-subtle hints about his need for a gun. And he closed his ears to another tale involving Misty's rumoured possession of a ruby necklace. Neither did he acknowledge Patrick when he offered congratulations on the speed of his working. Nor did he eat the meal Verna brought out for him.

It was only when he sensed that Misty was standing by his side did he slow his building and realize just how long into the night it was. He glanced at her and cracked a smile.

'You coming to do your praying?' he asked.

'Yes,' she snapped, her eyes blazing. 'But what did you say to Chase?'

'He told me to leave his store. So I went without complaint.' Dalton patted his pocket. 'I ain't complaining when he pays me in full.'

'I don't mean about your employment. I mean about me.'

For long moments Dalton didn't reply, but then shrugged and slammed a fist into his other palm.

'I just told him not to hit you no more.'

Misty winced. 'But I told you not to interfere.'

'But I couldn't leave Harmony without stopping him beating you.'

'You could. What exactly did you threaten him with?'

'I told him that I'd return to Harmony one day and if he'd hurt you while I was gone, I'd kill him.'

'And will you return?'

'Nope.'

'So it was just a hollow threat?'

'Chase ain't to know I'll never return.'

'He isn't that stupid.'

Dalton hung his head a moment, sighing.

'Perhaps not. Are you saying he beat you tonight?'

'No. But what he did was even worse.' Misty turned to stare into Harmony. A shiver rippled across her shoulders making her wrap her shawl across her chest. 'He has a blank look in his eyes and I just reckon that he'll keep bottling up his anger until he explodes. When he does, you won't be here to stop him. And I won't survive.'

'Then leave Harmony, or just leave him.'

'You don't understand. I can't leave.'

'Is it because you still love him? Because he don't deserve that.'

'No. Women don't leave their man.'

Dalton snorted. 'Then perhaps you should be the first.'

'I can't. I just can't. You don't understand.'

'Is it because he has a hold on you?' Dalton said, his voice low and guarded. 'Perhaps he has something of yours, something valuable.'

'Something . . . You're just like all the rest,' Misty screeched, then bit her bottom lip, her eyes watering. Then she swirled round on the spot and scurried into the church, her skirts swinging so much she almost trapped them in the door before she slammed it shut behind her.

Dalton tipped back his hat, irritated with himself for ruining his one chance to ask Misty about the necklace by asking in such an unsubtle way. But with no way to rectify his mistake now, he returned to completing his building.

Each previous time that Misty had entered the church, Dalton had retired before she emerged, but with his desire to finish the work by tomorrow, he kept working long into the night.

Even so, he guessed it was after midnight when she emerged. She just glanced at him, her eyes cold, reflective surfaces in the dark, then hurried into town.

Dalton placed a last rock on the wall, then sauntered into the church.

Patrick was kneeling before the altar with his hands clasped and his lips mouthing a silent prayer.

Dalton paced down the aisle, ensuring his footfalls were loud enough to alert him.

Patrick rose and turned to Dalton.

'Have you come to pray?' he asked, flashing a smile.

'No. Praying ain't no use.'

'That is not an opinion I share.'

'Then you reckon praying can stop

Chase beating Misty?'

'I pray every night that he will.'

'And every night he beats her.'

'He does. But I reckon your threats to Chase will be even less effective than my praying has been.'

Dalton ground his fist into his palm. 'Perhaps I just didn't threaten him enough. But I know one thing for sure, praying harder won't help her.'

Patrick stared at Dalton, then shrugged and turned to the altar.

'You cannot know for sure unless you have tried it. Recently, I prayed for a miracle and I received an answer.'

Dalton pointed a firm finger at Patrick, then shook his head and lowered his hand.

'We could argue about this forever but I'll never agree with you. But either way, I'm leaving tomorrow and I reckon that Misty will need someone to look out for her.'

Patrick turned to his room, then shrugged and turned back to face Dalton.

'Don't worry. I will continue to do that.'

'But I reckon she might need something more effective than praying. Ain't there something called sanctuary?'

'There is.' Patrick sighed. 'But I hope it won't come to that.'

Dalton nodded, then bade Patrick goodnight and sauntered outside. Within the head-high walls of the annex, he stretched, but as he spread out his blanket he heard a footfall crunch on gravel nearby and he edged into the doorway to look outside.

For a moment he saw nobody, but then, at the corner of the church wall, he saw Misty lurking in the shadows, watching him, her eyes bright in the darkness.

'What do you want?' he said, keeping his voice low.

Misty put a finger to her lips and beckoned Dalton to approach. With a shrug, Dalton paced from the doorway to join her.

'I've been thinking about your confrontation with Chase,' she said, her voice softer than it had been earlier. 'So I returned to — '

'If you here to apologize, don't. I should be the one to do that. I was trying to make things better, but I realize now that I was wrong.'

'But you were right. Threats are all a man like Chase understands and no matter how much I pray with Patrick, the beatings won't stop.'

'I wish I could help more. But tomorrow I'm leaving.'

'I know.' Misty stared at the church, then turned to him, her eyes large pools in the night. And when she spoke her lips were moist and her voice was even softer. 'But I also think you could leave having ensured that Chase never hurts me again.'

Dalton narrowed his eyes. 'What you saying?'

'I'm saying you reckon that Chase has my . . . he has something of mine, something valuable.'

Dalton nodded and turned from Misty to stare into the star-filled sky and for just a moment a bright star twinkled with a deep red glow.

'Do you mean the ruby necklace?'

'I do. But the tales Santiago has told you are wrong. Chase isn't keeping it from me. I'm keeping it from him. That's how the beatings started. If I tell him where I've hidden it, he's promised me that he'll stop, but I don't believe him.'

'You're right not to, but I still ain't sure what you're saying.'

'So you like plain speaking.' Misty stared at Dalton until he turned his gaze from the night sky. 'If you stop Chase ever beating me again, I'll give you the necklace.'

'You mean kill him?'

'If that is what it takes.'

'And you're prepared to give up something that valuable?'

'The necklace has brought me nothing but pain.' She rubbed her arm, wincing. 'The only times I dare wear it are late at night when nobody can see me. I haven't seen it in daylight in a year.'

Dalton searched Misty's large eyes, reading in them her years of suffering, but he tore his gaze away and looked to the sky. Even then, he had to force himself to look away from the star with the hint of redness.

'I'm sorry, Misty. You've misunderstood me. In my time I have done questionable things. And perhaps I could kill Chase in anger for what he's done to you, but I couldn't kill a man in cold blood for money.'

'He isn't worth calling a man.' Misty slapped a hand on Dalton's arm and even through the cloth, the warmth of her hand invaded his skin. 'And if you won't help me, I'll have to turn to someone else, perhaps even Milo. He's already offered to do it for a price a lot less than a ruby necklace.' She shivered and released her hand to wrap her shawl more tightly around her shoulders. 'And I can provide that if I must.'

She turned and paced from the church.

Unbidden, Dalton rested a hand on his arm where she had touched him and shivered too.

9

After a restless night, Dalton woke two hours before first light to ensure he completed the wall that morning. When the wall was a foot above his head, he declared the job complete and headed into town. With his collar turned high, he skirted round the backs of the buildings.

Fifty yards behind the saloon, he stopped and glanced left and right, confirming that he could see nobody outside, then knelt beside an old rabbit burrow and reached inside. He extracted the small bag, which contained the money he'd stolen from Chase, and slipped it into his pocket, then headed for the back of the saloon and around the side.

Again, he roved his gaze down the road, searching for Milo, and on confirming the road was deserted, headed into the saloon.

Santiago was the only customer. With his back to the door, he mopped up the greasy remnants of his breakfast with a heel of bread. At his feet, the two boys chomped on a hunk of bread. But on hearing footsteps Santiago turned, gave a cheery smile, and urged Dalton to join him.

Dalton shook his head and beckoned Santiago to follow him outside.

Santiago rubbed a finger along his moustache then wandered outside, wolfing down the bread while still managing to smile.

In the alley beside the saloon Dalton waited, standing so that he was hidden from casual interest but still able to see enough of the road and spot anyone who approached.

'What do you want?' Santiago asked, a huge grin on his lips.

'You said that you could get a man anything he wants.'

'I did — several times. But you just weren't interested.'

'I am now. I'd like a gun and a horse, by noon.'

'I can get you that.' Santiago spread his hands wide and grinned. 'It will cost fifty dollars.'

'I don't have fifty dollars.'

'Then we can't do business.'

Santiago turned to head towards the saloon, but Dalton grabbed his arm and pulled him back.

'Fifty dollars is too high. My best offer is ten now and ten more when I have the gun and horse.'

'You have a need. I am the only person offering a gun and a horse. I can't miss such an opportunity.' Santiago considered Dalton's firm jaw. 'But as I like you, Dalton, I'm prepared to drop my price by ten dollars.'

Dalton fixed Santiago with a firm gaze. 'I ain't in a position to bargain with you. I only have twenty dollars.'

'You are in a position of extreme weakness and you're trying to negotiate with an expert in the art. No matter what you claim, I know you stole fifty dollars from Chase.' Santiago watched Dalton curl his upper lip in a sneer, then lowered his head and sighed. 'But then again, perhaps Chase is as big a liar as they say he is and perhaps he didn't have that much money to steal.'

'Perhaps.'

Santiago raised his head and smiled. 'I will get you a horse and a gun. But the people I will buy from will need the twenty dollars before they hand over the goods.'

'Understood.'

Dalton reached into his pocket and extracted his wad of notes, but Santiago slammed a hand on his arm.

'But for you,' Santiago whispered, 'I will waive the charge.'

'You will?' Dalton sighed as he shrugged from Santiago's grip. 'Why do I not feel obliged?'

'Because you are a clever man and because you have guessed that I will waive the charge only if you comply with my conditions.'

'Which are?'

'You wish to leave Harmony and then hide. But you don't know this area and you don't know where to hide. But I can help you hide somewhere where Milo Bunch and even Walker Dodge won't find you.'

'Milo might still bear a grudge against me, but why would a lawman track me down?'

'Because you have committed a crime. Because you have something he wants. Or maybe just because he's a mean varmint.'

'For twenty dollars, no lawman will waste his time.'

'For twenty dollars, he won't.' Santiago glanced around the alley to peer up and down the deserted road, then leaned to Dalton and lowered his voice. 'But for a ruby necklace, he'll chase you to the ends of the Earth.'

'I don't have the necklace.'

'Maybe not yet, but you will have once you've killed Chase.'

Dalton bit his bottom lip, trying and failing to hide his discomfort, but as

Santiago grinned, he nodded.

'How do you know about that?'

'Because you ain't the first man Misty has asked to kill her husband.'

Dalton closed his eyes a moment. 'She said that Milo offered to do it, but she refused when she didn't like his price.'

'Is that what she told you?' Santiago snorted. 'Milo says it was *him* who refused *her* offer.'

'I wouldn't believe a word Milo says. It's more likely that he just didn't have the guts.'

'Perhaps, but before he did it, I reckon he saw something he liked even more than Misty — the ruby necklace.'

Dalton blew out his cheeks. 'And has she asked you to kill Chase?'

'No, but if you don't do it, I might be next. There aren't that many suitable men in town.'

'Has she asked Patrick?'

'Don't know, but he's been suffering something awful for weeks. I reckon that at the very least she's testing his faith.' Santiago raised his eyebrows. 'So, do you want to hear my conditions?'

Dalton kicked at the ground, then paced round to face Santiago. He forced the most placid and innocent expression he could manage and held his hands wide.

'I'll tell you this one last time. I do not intend to kill Chase. I am not searching for the necklace. I just want to leave town before Walker Dodge returns. I'd walk but Milo is determined to kill me and what with Misty drawing me into something I don't want to get involved in, I need to defend myself and get away quickly. So I need a horse and a gun.'

Santiago stared deep into Dalton's eyes, narrowing his own eyes to slits as he appeared to search deep into Dalton's mind. Dalton didn't blink and after what seemed an eternity, Santiago glanced away.

'All right,' he whispered. 'But if that is true, all you will get is a horse and a gun.'

Santiago held out a hand and Dalton slapped his twenty dollars into it.

Dalton watched Santiago mount his horse and gallop out of town, then headed back to the church, taking a direct route down the centre of the road.

As he walked, he pondered the tangle of conflicting stories he'd heard over the last week and from them tried to unravel which snippets of information he could trust.

He decided that Misty was strong-willed and that meant her offer to him was plausible, although whether she would relinquish the necklace after he'd killed Chase, he didn't know.

But Dalton had no intention of finding out.

Even for a reward as fabulous as the ruby necklace, he couldn't kill a man, even one as worthless as Chase.

But that didn't stop him wondering where Misty had hidden it.

As Misty rarely left the house, she had few options for a hiding place that

Chase wouldn't find. Her unsubtle hints about the price Milo wanted, her seeming warmth towards Dalton, and her comment about her bedroom being the one place Chase wouldn't go, suggested a possible hiding place.

But Dalton didn't trust the word of someone who was prepared to hire him to kill another person, and that meant she had to have hidden it somewhere else.

And almost certainly that was outside the house.

With this in mind, a sudden thought hit him and with a smile on his lips, he entered the church, but as Verna and Patrick were inside making breakfast, he wandered outside. He fussed over his building work and tidied away the unused rocks until breakfast was ready.

After eating, he offered to clean the dishes so that Patrick and Verna could leave for their daily rounds earlier than normal, and assured Patrick that he would still be here when he returned.

They left, beaming with delight.

Alone, he washed the plates, then headed to the door to check that they had gone. Then he stood with his back to the door and gazed around the interior of the church.

The only place that Misty visited outside her home was the church. But as he reckoned that Patrick was incapable of duplicity that meant Misty had hidden the necklace without his help.

And that meant the hiding place was a good one, but also accessible.

He paced around the church, tapping the solid walls. They were stone and had no furniture near them aside from the rough altar and the rows of pews. Even so, Dalton lifted each piece of furniture, then replaced it on the same spot. He even lifted the cross and peered beneath.

He stood at the altar and gazed at the roof, then at the floor. The roof was high and solid, the floor was scuffed earth, and any recent digging would be easily visible.

Two rooms veered off from the church on either side of the altar. He opened the door to the first and peered inside. This was Patrick's room. It had a blanket on the floor atop straw bedding. The only other items were a bible and a water jug and bowl.

With guilt warming his cheeks, Dalton ruffled the straw but beneath he only found scuffed earth. Patrick had raised the earth to provide him with a drier place to sleep, but aside from that, the room was bare.

One last time he glanced around the room, then headed out and across the church to the room opposite.

This room contained the table, around which they ate, and a cupboard.

Dalton threw open the doors to the cupboard. He peered at the heap of utensils, then shaking his head, threw the doors closed, but just as the doors slammed to, something on the back wall caught his gaze.

Dalton opened the doors again and hunkered down.

The cupboard lacked a back and behind a bowl, the mortar around the lowest stone block in the wall was missing.

Dalton pushed the bowl and utensils to one side, prised his fingers around the edge of the stone, and pulled. Far more easily than he expected, the stone slipped out and slammed on to the cupboard bottom.

He peered inside the hole, but saw only dry pellets, perhaps rodent dropping. Without much hope, he levered his arm in and felt around, finding nothing but the back wall of what he judged to be a two foot square space behind the stone.

Dalton levered the stone back into place and replaced the utensils as he thought they had been lying previously.

He scratched his chin as he stood. This hiding place was such an obvious place for Misty to have hidden the necklace. It seemed to have existed since the church was built and someone hadn't just scraped away the mortar recently. And the cupboard could have stood anywhere in the room, but it stood before this hiding place.

But then again, he surmised, the church was symmetrical.

He paced from the inner wall to the missing stone, counting fifteen stone blocks.

Then he dashed to Patrick's room. He stood by the inner wall and counted fifteen stone blocks from the wall to mirror the location of the hollowed out space in the facing room.

The fifteenth block that was level with the ground did not have missing mortar.

Dalton hung his head a moment, but then knelt and glanced along the row of stone blocks, finding that Patrick's bedding and mound of raised earth hid the bottom layer of stone blocks.

Although Dalton guessed that Patrick's return was close, this was the last chance he'd have for searching and so he knelt on Patrick's bedding and paddled the earth away. Within a few handfuls he'd scraped away a foot of earth and as he hoped, the revealed wall had the same stone without mortar.

Dalton increased the speed of his scraping until he had cleared a gap around the block. Dalton rolled his shoulders, then tugged on the block.

This block was tighter than the block in the other room, almost as if it had rarely been removed.

And when he'd pulled it all the way out, lying in the shadows inside was a wooden box. Intricate carvings graced the sides. Gilt edged the lid. And set within an engraved circle on the lid was a single gemstone.

With his hands shaking, Dalton reached for the box, but just as his fingers brushed the wood, the church door creaked open.

10

Dalton wavered, one hand questing for the lock even as with the other hand, he reached for the stone block.

But having found where Misty had hidden the necklace, he decided to leave it in its current hiding place rather than search for somewhere else to keep it until he had the means to leave in a hurry.

As footfalls shuffled down the aisle, he scraped the stone back into place, then shovelled the earth back on top.

In the church the footsteps stopped before the altar.

With the extra time, Dalton flattened the earth with his heels, then scuffed it back and forth with his sole to remove his scrapings and placed the straw back on the raised bed.

Then he edged to the door and

listened. Outside, he heard low breathing. Whether it was from Patrick or someone else, he couldn't tell.

As Dalton couldn't think of a valid lie to explain why he was in Patrick's quarters, he stayed where he was, but then in the church the main door slammed back, the sound echoing.

'Help,' Misty screeched from inside the church.

'What's wrong?' Patrick said, his voice coming from the doorway.

'Chase is looking for me. And he's mighty annoyed.'

'What set him off?'

'Dalton warned Chase not to hurt me yesterday, but that's enflamed him. If I hadn't have ran, I don't know what he'd have done.'

'You're safe here. Chase will never come in here.'

'I hope you're right. But I'm worried about Dalton too. He did what he thought was right, but Chase has a rifle and he's all set to kill him.'

'I'll find Verna and tell her to keep

away. And I'll find Chase and talk to him. You stay here.'

'Don't look for him,' Misty whined. 'Dalton can take care of himself. You can't.'

'The Lord will protect me. And if he doesn't . . . I will be fine.'

The church door closed.

Dalton listened at the door, but all he heard was a low murmuring so he edged the door open a fraction.

In the church, Misty was kneeling before the altar and praying to herself. She'd clamped her eyes shut and clutched her hands so tightly that she'd drained all the blood from them.

As Dalton saw no reason to suppose that she'd been lying, he swung the door open, ensuring it creaked.

Misty started, leaping to her feet with a hand bolting to her mouth, but she couldn't stop a scream ripping from her throat.

'Don't worry,' Dalton said. 'It's just me.'

'What were you doing in there?'

Misty murmured, her voice breathless as she placed a hand to her chest.

'Sleeping. All that building was tiring.' Dalton suppressed a fake yawn. 'Where did you last see Chase?'

'In the store, but I don't reckon he's there now.'

Dalton leaned back against the doorway and searched her eyes but detected only fright and perhaps concern for his safety.

'And what caused his anger?' he asked. 'What happened that you can't tell Patrick?'

'If you were listening, you heard it all. And he is mighty angry.'

Dalton shrugged. 'Then I'll have to find him and calm him down.'

'Or not,' Misty whispered.

'Stop thinking like that and go back to your praying.' Dalton pulled his hat low and headed down the aisle.

Misty called after him, beseeching him to stay in the church, but Dalton set his shoulders high and stormed through the door.

He maintained a firm pace until he reached Harmony. There, he set his legs wide and gazed at each building in turn, but the road was deserted.

He headed on to the boardwalk, but even with his truculent attitude, when he came to Chase's store, he crawled on hands and knees past the windows, then stood and headed for the saloon.

At the door, he strained his hearing, listening for anyone talking inside the saloon.

He detected two low voices. One was the bartender, but he didn't recognize the other. He guessed that it wouldn't be Chase — he wouldn't be keeping quiet as he searched for him.

A hand slammed on his shoulder and swung him round. A bunched fist smashed into his jaw, slamming him back against the saloon wall.

Dalton shook his head and staggered from the wall only to receive another blow to the cheek that knocked him to his knees.

He bent down with his head hung,

but a kick to the guts bundled him into the alley. Dalton rolled from his assailant's flailing boot, then staggered to his feet and righted himself.

He faced back down the alley to see Milo smirking at him and flexing his fist.

'Told you to stay out of town,' Milo muttered. 'Seems some people just don't listen to sense.'

'I'm leaving, Milo, just as soon as I've seen Santiago.'

'You are leavin'. But you're doin' it now.'

Dalton glanced at Milo's waist, which lacked a gunbelt.

'You ain't packing a gun. Guess I was right and you ain't got the guts to follow through with your threats.'

'I have got the guts.' Milo swung back his fist and advanced down the alley. 'I just reckon I'll enjoy myself first.'

Dalton backed a pace, forcing Milo to advance even further. Milo swaggered to him, then hurled another punch at Dalton's face, but Dalton ducked under it and bundled into Milo with his shoulder, pushing him back against the wall.

Milo flailed his fists, but with Dalton holding him in a firm bear hug, Milo couldn't get the leverage to deliver anything more than soft blows to his arms.

Milo relented from his assault and tried to squirm from Dalton's grip, but Dalton only wrapped his arms even more tightly around Milo's chest and, as he closed his fists behind Milo's back, flexed his shoulders and squeezed.

Milo gasped and wriggled as Dalton gripped with all his might. In desperation Milo pushed from the wall and tried to walk Dalton back towards the opposite side of the alley.

Dalton thrust his feet wide and stood his ground.

Milo gasped and whined in his ear, but just as Dalton heard Milo's breath become ragged, he released him with a sudden snap of his arms. Suddenly free,

Milo staggered back a pace and, taking advantage of his winded confusion, Dalton rocked back his fist and thundered it into Milo's guts.

Milo folded over the blow and Dalton slammed a sharp uppercut to his chin that rocked him back on his heels and slammed his head into the wall.

Milo slid down the wall, but Dalton grabbed his collar and stopped him falling. He hoisted him high and slammed a solid blow deep into his guts.

Dalton rocked back his fist. 'Enough?'

'Get off me,' Milo murmured, his voice ragged.

'Sounds like you ain't had enough.'

Dalton released his grip and hurled back his fist, then slammed a long round-armed blow to Milo's jaw that lifted his feet off the ground before he slammed into the wall and slid to the ground.

Dalton reached down and grabbed Milo's collar. He hoisted him up, but

Milo raised a limp hand.

'Enough,' he whispered.

'Not loud enough,' Dalton muttered, hurling back his fist.

'That's enough,' Milo screeched.

Dalton grinned. 'That's loud enough.'

Dalton dragged Milo to his feet and pushed him down the alley, but Milo stumbled to a standstill, then staggered round on the spot to glare at Dalton.

'But this ain't over, Dalton.'

Dalton nodded and advanced a long pace on Milo with a fist raised.

'If you insist.'

Milo glanced at the fist, then hurtled from the alley and into the road.

For a few half-hearted paces Dalton chased Milo, but slid to a halt when he realized that he'd let Chase see him if he was on the road, and edged back into the alley.

Milo wheeled his arms as he searched for more speed, but then slid to a halt and staggered round in the centre of the road.

'I'm waitin' for you, Dalton,' he

shouted, his voice echoing down the road. He kicked at the earth, sending up huge plumes of dirt.

Dalton glanced at the buildings nearest to Milo, wondering whether Milo's ambush was just a decoy to entice him out for Chase to get him, or whether Milo was just fighting his own battle. Either way, he decided Milo's display was sure to attract Chase before too much longer.

'All right,' Dalton muttered and stormed into the road with a fist raised.

Milo glared at him, but when Dalton was within five paces of him, he swirled round and dashed down the road.

Dalton hurtled after him, slamming his feet to the ground and kicking dust at his back, but Milo redoubled his speed and surged beyond the edge of town and down the trail. His legs whirled as he built enough momentum to look as if he could run all the way to Rock Ridge.

Dalton slid to a halt and stopped,

watching Milo with a smile on his lips, then turned.

In the centre of the road facing him a lone rider stood.

11

Dalton flinched, but then realized the new arrival was Santiago. He glanced along the road, confirming that Chase wasn't around, then dashed to Santiago's side.

'Where's my horse?' he asked.

'I have it. And a gun.' Santiago grinned. 'But just how badly do — '

Dalton grabbed Santiago's leg and with a firm gesture, yanked him from the saddle.

Santiago hit the ground heavily and rolled, but when he came up, Dalton grabbed his collar and pulled him up to stare into his eyes.

'You reckon that you have me where you want me, but I ain't negotiating the price. Twenty dollars is every last cent I own.' Dalton pushed Santiago to the ground and dragged out the lining of his pockets. 'I got nothing left.'

Santiago glanced at the pockets, then shrugged.

'Except for a few thousand dollars, maybe more if the rubies are as fabulous as Milo says they are.'

'I don't have the necklace,' Dalton grunted through gritted teeth.

Santiago's eyes opened wide. 'And you are lying.'

'You got no proof and you'll never get any. So, just tell me where you've left my horse and gun and I'll leave you to claim the necklace when you decide to do Misty's bidding.'

'I have something better than proof. I understand you. And you wouldn't run scared just because of the likes of Milo.'

'Walker Dodge will return soon, perhaps even today. And I ain't got a gun. He has.' Dalton lunged for Santiago's collar, but Santiago shuffled back, his grip closing on air. Dalton shrugged and bunched a fist. 'And no matter how tough you reckon I am, I don't like those odds. But if you don't tell me where you've left my horse, I will show you what I can do with my fists.'

Santiago just smiled. 'You won't hit me. You're a man who ends fights, but doesn't start them.'

'You reckon you know me well.' Dalton rolled his shoulders and swung back his fist. 'But I've already given Milo a good thrashing today, and you're next if you don't start talking.'

'I will talk, but not about your horse. You see I also reckon you'd judge the risk from Milo and Walker as something you could deal with when you're close to the necklace.' Santiago smiled. 'And as you haven't killed Chase, the only reason you'd leave is because you've found it.'

Dalton glared at Santiago then, with a snap of his wrist, relaxed his fists.

'I ain't got no necklace,' he muttered, standing back to stare down the deserted road. He lowered his voice to a resigned murmur. 'But just to end your whining, what are you trying to gain out of this?'

Santiago rubbed his thin moustache and knelt.

'You've found where Chase has hidden Misty's necklace. And now you have to escape. You need a horse, but when Chase discovers that the necklace is gone he'll let everyone know what happened and everyone, including me, will chase after you. You can avoid most of us, but not Walker Dodge. To escape him, you need help.'

'And from your smug grin I guess you're offering to provide me with a way to escape.'

Santiago rolled to his feet and edged round to stand beside Dalton. He grabbed his horse's reins and draped his other arm around Dalton's shoulders. At a steady pace he walked him down the road. Only when they were beyond the last building and standing fifty yards before the church, did he stop.

'For fifty per cent of a ruby necklace,

I'll take you anywhere you want to go and provide you with anything you want.'

'And if I don't have a ruby necklace?'

'Then the first man that tracks you down gets one hundred percent of the necklace. And I know this area better than anyone, including Walker Dodge, so that'll be me.'

Dalton shrugged Santiago's arm from his shoulder.

'And if I did have it, you reckon that you could take me on when you found me?'

'Perhaps not. But for a cut of my profits I could hire the likes of Milo and a few others like him. And they could deal with you.' Santiago fingered his moustache. 'But it doesn't have to be that way.'

'It does. Because if you do find me, you'll disappoint all the people you've promised a cut when you find I ain't got no necklace.' Dalton slammed his hands on his hips and hunched forward, glaring at Santiago. But when

Santiago just returned a level gaze, he stood back. 'But I ain't got time for games, Santiago. Just tell me where you left my horse.'

Santiago shrugged. 'If that is how you want to deal with this — in one hour head down the gully. I will have left the horse and the gun beside Baxter's Rock — it's a large outcrop, two miles out. You can't miss it.'

'Obliged.'

'Don't be. I can follow tracks. You won't get far before I find you.'

'And don't disappoint me. If that horse ain't there, it won't be long before I find you.'

Dalton tipped his hat and turned. With his head down, he strode towards the church.

'The horse will be there, Dalton,' Santiago called after him. 'But twenty dollars was such a low price, I hope that the horse ain't so old that it'll keel over after the first mile, or that the gun ain't too rusty to fire.'

Dalton gritted his teeth and strode

another ten paces, but then slowed to a halt and turned. From under a lowered hat he stared at Santiago then, shaking his head, wandered back.

'I'll give you twenty per cent,' he whispered.

Dalton searched Santiago's eyes for a hint of triumph, but if anything, he only detected disappointment.

'You caved in easier than I expected. But no. I get either fifty percent or one hundred per cent.'

'Twenty-five.'

Santiago shook his head. 'I have negotiated deals for whole days and nights over a single percentage point. You will not win with me. Just accept my offer and we can start this.'

'Thirty.'

'And how will you sell the necklace? It ain't something you can sell without creating fuss. You need to know what to do with it. And the extra price you'll get with my help might double what you'll get without my help.'

Dalton tipped back his hat. 'All right. Fifty per cent.'

'Deal.'

Santiago moved to mount his horse, but Dalton slammed a hand on his shoulder.

'But I'm getting to think that a man with as many talents as you might have ideas of his own about the necklace.'

Santiago slipped from under Dalton's hand and mounted his horse.

'You're right not to trust me. But I got no desire to double-cross you. I reckon we make a good team.' Santiago chuckled. 'Come on. We have some hard riding ahead of us.'

Santiago reached down to help Dalton up on to his horse, but Dalton shook his head.

'I don't have the necklace on me. It's in a safe place. Head to Baxter's Rock as before, and I'll see you there in an hour.'

'Agreed,' Santiago said, 'partner.'

Dalton held his arm to the side to gesture down the road to the open trail beyond.

'Agreed, partner.'

12

When Santiago had left town, Dalton dashed to the church. But when he threw back the door, Misty was standing before the altar. She started, then swirled round and raised her eyebrows on seeing that it was Dalton.

'Dalton,' she shouted, scurrying down the aisle towards him. 'You're safe. And Chase?'

'I didn't see him,' Dalton said. 'He must be out of town searching the trails for me.'

'Then, when he returns . . . '

'When he returns, I won't be doing nothing but talking to him, then leaving town.' Dalton glanced over Misty's shoulder at Patrick's room. 'So get some coffee brewing and relax.'

Misty nodded and headed to the stove in the side room, but just as Dalton turned towards Patrick's room, the church door opened and Patrick dashed in.

Dalton slapped a fist against his thigh, then slumped on to the front pew, abandoning his plan to get the necklace, for now.

Once the breathless Patrick was satisfied that Dalton hadn't found and dealt with Chase, he settled down with Dalton, then Misty on the front pew. While drinking two rounds of coffee, they shared animated conversation about where Chase might be and what he might do when he returned.

Misty started whenever she heard a noise and Patrick repeatedly encouraged Dalton to join in him praying for deliverance from Chase's anger. But Dalton avoided answering and instead racked his mind for a valid excuse to send them both away so that he could retrieve the box.

But everything that he thought of saying only sounded suspicious when he rehearsed it in his mind.

Then a fist pounded on the door,

interrupting his pondering.

'I know you're in there, Dalton,' a voice, clearly Chase's, shouted from the doorway.

Misty flinched and cowered before the altar, but Patrick patted her shoulder.

'Don't worry,' he said. 'Chase won't come in here.'

'Come out, Dalton!' Chase demanded. 'I got me a rifle to take you on.'

Patrick gulped. 'But to avoid trouble, it seems we'll have to prove to Chase that Dalton isn't here.'

Dalton shrugged. 'But how can — '

Patrick put a finger to his lips and shepherded Dalton into the left-hand side room. Dalton let Patrick lead him and to Patrick's directions, helped drag the cupboard four feet to the side.

On the revealed ground was a trapdoor. Dalton sighed on realizing that the cupboard was covering this escape route and not the hollowed out space in the wall.

'It comes out twenty yards from the church,' Patrick said. 'Just hide until we've proved to Chase that you've gone. Don't worry. I can end this without violence if you're not here.'

Dalton nodded and lifted the door. Below, stone steps headed into the darkness. He tipped his hat to Patrick.

Misty stood a foot back from him, a mixture of questioning and pleading furrowing her brow.

Dalton glanced at Patrick's room, but then shrugged, deciding to again postpone retrieving the necklace, and just tipped his hat to her too and paced down the steps.

Even with Patrick leaving the trapdoor open the darkness beyond was absolute, so with his hands held out before him, he shuffled forward as quickly as he dared. The air was stale, roots flicked at his face, insects and rodents scurried over his feet, but he maintained his steady pace and after thirty paces, his questing foot barged against another stone step.

He climbed, his hands over his head and after four steps he hit the roof. In the darkness he fingered around and located the edges of a door.

He pushed but the door remained solid. He climbed another step and pushed harder, but still found no give. So, with the darkness and the rank air pressing him into the onset of panic, he climbed as high as possible and leant forward, pressing his back to the trapdoor, and pushed upwards.

For pained moments the trapdoor held, but then with a creak and a shower of dirt the trapdoor flew upwards, tumbling him out on to the ground.

As promised he was twenty yards from the back of the church, behind the remnants of the wall.

Dalton listened to Chase slamming his fist on the church door, then swung the trapdoor closed. He scraped a few swipes of dirt over the door to hide it from casual interest, then hurried to the dry gully.

He slid down the bank and sat a moment, gathering his breath, then scurried on hands and feet back to the top and peered at the church.

He could still hear Chase's taunts, so he slid to the bottom and stretched his back, then headed away from town at a steady trot. With the rainfall having been limited recently, the base of the gully was dry and stony and Dalton made good time.

But as the rendezvous point with Santiago was two miles out of town, even the weak sun raised a thick sweat on his brow. And within ten minutes Dalton regretted not agreeing to meet in a place that was nearer to town.

When the gully opened out on to a river, Dalton caught his breath.

Last week this was where Walker Dodge had bushwhacked him and, after escaping, he had made the crucial decision to walk up the dry gully rather than following the river — a decision that had probably saved his life.

He climbed to the top of the bank

and peered around.

About a half-mile further on, a tangle of trees nestled before a sentinel rock. This was the only landmark and had to be Baxter's Rock.

With his eyes narrowed, Dalton reckoned that he could see two horses and maybe a figure. He jumped on the spot, waving his hands above his head, but if it was a figure by the tree, it didn't see him. And not daring to risk whistling, he hurried to a fast trot.

After five minutes of running he was level with the trees, and veered out on to the plains, slowing to catch his breath.

Two horses were before the largest rock but the figure that he reckoned was Santiago was now just a bush.

But Santiago had to be close.

Dalton ran his gaze over the thick tangle of trees and then over the outcropping of rock behind, but the only movement came from the tethered horses standing beside the outlying trees.

‘Santiago,’ he called, slowing to a halt fifty yards from the trees. ‘Come on. I’m exhausted.’

He stood with his hands on his knees, dragging full breaths into his lungs, but when no reply emerged from ahead, he resumed walking.

In a wide arc, he edged round to face the outlying trees, and as more of the ground appeared beyond the trees, he saw Santiago sitting back against a tree with his head slumped on his chest.

‘Come on, Santiago,’ he shouted. ‘This ain’t the time or the weather for a siesta.’

Still walking towards him, Dalton narrowed his eyes, but when Santiago continued to lie back against the tree, Dalton stopped.

He edged ten yards to his side and with Santiago in full view, he could see that he wasn’t sleeping. Santiago lay sprawled, his legs wide and his head lolling.

And worse, a bloom of blood had exploded across his jacket.

Dalton closed his eyes a moment, then swirled round.

From behind the rock, Milo stepped out, a lively grin on his face and his gun aimed at Dalton's head.

'That's far enough, Dalton,' he said.

Dalton stood tall. He had seen a gun lying at Santiago's side so he put his weight on his right foot, ready to run for it.

'Didn't think you'd have the guts to take anyone on, Milo. But you'll regret it.'

'Wrong on both counts. I didn't kill Santiago, and I intend to enjoy this.' Milo stepped to the side and from behind the rock three riders paced out.

Each rider was hard-boned and cold-eyed. And they all wore a badge — Sheriff Walker Dodge and his deputies, Vaughn and Hayden.

In unison the three lawmen raised their guns to aim them at Dalton's head.

'Dalton,' Walker muttered, 'give me the necklace, or die.'

13

Dalton raised his hands, a resigned smile on his face, but as Walker gestured for the deputies to seize him, Dalton swung round and dashed away from them.

He guessed that they'd expect him to run for the horses and maybe Santiago's gun, but he ignored both opportunities and hurtled towards the river instead.

Behind him, Walker barked command to everyone and within seconds, hoofs thundered as the lawmen galloped after him, but Dalton thrust his head down and headed for the river.

The hoof beats pounded closer and closer but just as Dalton guessed they were within yards of him, he reached the bank, threw his arms up, and dived into the river.

The cold water slapped into his face, but he forced down an urge to gasp as his high dive swooped him straight to the bottom. For two long strokes, he swam towards the opposite bank before he let the water buoy him up to the surface.

With a shake of his head to free his eyes of water, he swung round to face the lawmen, treading water.

The line of riders spread out along the bank and faced him. With a short gesture, Walker ordered Deputy Vaughn to head upriver and Deputy Hayden to head downriver. Milo reached the bank edge but Walker kept his gaze set forward, not even acknowledging his presence.

Dalton watched them spread out, confirming that they were planning to outflank him.

He swam in a circle and glanced at the opposite bank, but from what he remembered, the hills, and perhaps a place to hide, were a good mile away. And ahead, the river had numerous shallow patches across which a horse could cross without the rider getting his boots wet. So even if Walker didn't want to swim across, if he headed for the opposite bank, he wouldn't run far before Walker caught him.

So he had to stay in the water.

He swam back in a circle to face Walker again.

By now, Vaughn and Hayden had spread out to fifty yards beyond him and had stopped to watch him.

'Dalton,' Walker shouted, 'you ain't escaping this time.'

Dalton gritted his teeth on hearing this truth. But unlike the last time when he'd dived into the river, none of the lawmen had fired at him, and that meant they were determined to take him alive.

The river was around fifteen feet deep and if they weren't going to shoot him, they'd have to come in and get him and that wouldn't be easy. On the other hand the chill was creeping into Dalton's fingers and toes and he reckoned he had ten minutes before he'd have to come out or freeze.

Still with no plan as to how he might escape, Dalton took a huge breath and dived underwater. He swam down to the bottom, then headed downriver, letting the current and his long strokes take him as far as possible.

He counted his strokes and on the twelfth stroke, the buzzing in his ears and the desperate desire for breath forced him to surface. In a shower of water he hit the surface and gasped for air as he glanced upriver.

Deputy Hayden was ten yards ahead of him. Walker Dodge was five yards back and trotting to catch up with him.

Upriver, Vaughn had followed him and was only twenty yards back, standing above a fallen tree tangled up with a collapsed length of bank.

Dalton took three long strokes downriver, and sure enough, the lawmen kept abreast of him, one ahead, one at his side, and one some yards back.

'Dalton,' Walker shouted, 'you're wasting time. Give up.'

Dalton considered his journey along

the riverbank and as far as he could remember, a shallow region was just beyond the next bend.

Keeping his head above water, Dalton dragged deep breaths into his lungs and angled his swimming towards the opposite bank, then dived again.

In two long strokes he swam to the bottom, but on noticing how murky the water was, in a sudden decision, he kicked off from the bottom and headed upriver instead.

He fought against the current, again counting his strokes. At twelve, he forced himself to stay below water and dragged another five strokes from his tiring limbs before his racked lungs forced him to head for the surface.

But despite the desire to hit the surface and gasp for air, he floated to the top and nudged his head above water and gulped a deep breath, then dived again.

He was beside the fallen tree and his pursuers were downriver, flanking the approximate position where he would be if he had headed with them. And they were looking downriver.

But even with this minimal advantage, he judged that wherever he headed he would only have a few seconds before they relocated him.

Dalton surfaced again, took a breath and dived. With no better idea coming to him, he swam underwater for the fallen tree. As silently as he could he surfaced and rolled between the branches without looking to see if Walker had seen him hide.

With a few firm kicks, he burrowed beneath the tree into the sticky mass of leaves and silt.

From down the river, the muffled voices of the lawmen and Milo sounded and from the angry tones they were now wondering why he hadn't surfaced.

Hidden in the sticky, acrid smelling mess, Dalton kept his breathing shallow and put all his hope into remaining undiscovered until his pursuers were far enough away that he could risk emerging to dash for Santiago's horses.

But this place was such an obvious place to hide.

Voices sounded nearby, at first muffled, although from their sharp tones Dalton detected their irritation. Then he heard individual words.

'Where is he?' Walker shouted.

'He has to come up somewhere,' Vaughn said.

'Perhaps he's drowned.'

'Then he'd float back up.'

'Hayden, get those horses. I reckon he's planning to reach them.'

Dalton winced as his only chance of escape disappeared. But he burrowed even deeper into the mess of river filth, hanging on to the pathetic hope that they wouldn't find him here.

Then the fallen tree above him shook as of somebody jumping on to it. Dalton cringed, hopelessly trying to make himself as small as possible.

Above him footsteps paced down the tree, the shaking freeing more filth for it to shower down on Dalton's head. Taking a risk, Dalton pushed a shoulder up against the tree and pushed. The tree only moved a fraction but a curse sounded from above and a splash when whoever was on the tree slipped and landed in the water.

More curses sounded, only feet to Dalton's side, but from up on the bank a peel of laughter sounded.

'Milo,' Walker roared, 'you're an idiot. Quit trying to drown yourself and find Dalton.'

Dalton took a deep breath, lowering his breathing and fighting down the first surge of hope that he could remain hidden.

Slithering sounded as Milo fought to climb the bank, but then another crash sounded as he failed and tumbled into the water.

Milo muttered and cursed as he dragged himself from the water, but then he grabbed the tree to help pull himself out. The tree shook as Milo staggered past Dalton's position.

Dalton pushed back, searching for another few inches of hiding space beneath the silt and river filth, but then Milo's grinning face appeared above him.

'He's here!' Milo shouted, gibbering his delight as he peered at Dalton.

Milo leaned in, a hand outstretched to grab Dalton's collar, but with pure rage coursing through his veins, Dalton hurled a fist at Milo's face. The fist only caught Milo a glancing blow, but even so, Milo tumbled on to his back.

Without a choice, Dalton hurtled out from under the tree in a shower of dirt. He grabbed Milo and threw him on to his side, but to his further irritation, Milo was no longer packing a gun.

Hoofs thundered down the bank behind him, but Dalton still patted Milo's jacket searching for a hidden gun. When he didn't find one, he bunched a fist and slugged Milo's chin, tumbling him into the river, then scurried up the bank.

Hayden was trotting away from him towards Baxter's Rock and the horses, cutting off his one hope of escape.

Vaughn and Walker were fifty yards to his side and galloping at him.

With a hopeless sickness in his guts, Dalton glanced at the river, but a shiver ripped through his muscles and he couldn't face leaping into the water again, so he turned and dashed down the side of the river.

Behind him hoofs pounded, and without hope, Dalton thrust his head down and hurtled, his arms wheeling as he fought for an extra burst of speed.

When he judged that the riders were five seconds away from flanking him, he accepted that he'd just have to suffer the cold again and threw his hands up, ready to leap into the river.

But then a tightness ripped across his chest and pulled him on his back.

He glanced down to see that Vaughn had lassoed him, the rope encasing his chest and pinning his upper arms to his side. With frantic gestures, he ripped at the bonds, but Vaughn pulled them tight and without a choice, he ceased his struggling and looked up at Vaughn, then at Walker.

'You have just irritated me, Dalton,' Walker muttered, holding out a hand. 'So you will give me the ruby necklace. Then I will kill you.'

14

Dalton rolled to his feet and flexed his back trying to loosen the tightness across his chest, but Vaughn tugged on the rope, tightening it even more. The sudden pressure forced Dalton to his knees and made him feel that he was in danger of being cut in two.

On the ground he settled for just glaring up at Walker.

'What necklace?' he grunted.

Walker shook his head. 'I can believe you're dumb, but you ain't good at playing dumb. So I'll say this one more time — give me the ruby necklace you've stolen from Chase Valdez.'

'That storekeeper ain't rich enough to own — '

'Enough!' Walker gestured to Deputy Hayden, who had just joined them. 'Search him.'

Hayden dismounted and sauntered

towards Dalton.

Dalton struggled to his feet and backed from him, but another sharp tug on the rope from Vaughn halted him.

'I ain't no thief,' Dalton said, levering his arms up at the elbow to hold them wide. 'You've got the wrong man.'

Hayden patted Dalton's pockets. His eyes widened and he ripped out a fold of bills.

'What's this?' he asked, grinning and holding the bills aloft.

'That's all the money I've got.' Dalton snorted. 'And it ain't enough to buy myself any kind of necklace, neither mind no ruby one.'

Hayden riffled through the bills. 'Six dollars.'

'That's some of the money he stole off Chase,' Milo shouted.

Walker leaned forward in the saddle. 'Seems like I've found a thief, after all. And I got every reason to string up a thief.'

'I earned that money working for Chase Valdez,' Dalton said.

'Six dollars,' Milo murmured with a snort. 'Chase ain't that generous for a week's work.'

'He promised more than a week's work, but he paid me for the whole time when he let me go early.'

Milo shook his head. 'That don't sound like Chase either.'

'It don't. Chase is a mean varmint who beats his wife. But when I told him to stop, he paid me to leave to avoid a beating from me.'

Walker dismounted and called his deputies into a huddle. As they shared low words, Milo swaggered to Dalton's side and looked him up and down, a smug grin on his face.

'If you tell Walker where it is,' he said, 'you might live.'

Dalton bunched his fists, but then forced them to slacken and smiled.

'Stop gloating. You and I have more in common than not.'

'I share nothin' with you.'

Dalton glanced at the lawmen, who were still muttering to each other, then lowered his voice.

'Misty duped us both. She offered to *reward* you if you killed Chase.'

Milo gulped. 'How did you know that?'

'Because she made me the same offer.'

'But she . . . ' Milo lowered his head, muttering to himself.

'You're a decent man.' Dalton coughed, forcing his voice to stay low and serious. 'You were tempted but you couldn't kill a man in cold blood, whatever the reward and however low the man. It's the same for me. I couldn't kill Chase either, so I'm leaving town and I'm never returning.'

As Milo kicked at the earth, muttering under his breath, Walker turned from his deputies and stalked to Dalton's side.

'So,' he said, 'you're saying you have no idea where the necklace is.'

Dalton turned from Milo and faced Walker.

'I haven't.'

Walker held out his hand for Vaughn to slap the rope into his grip. Then he ripped his gun from its holster and aimed it straight between Dalton's eyes.

'And that means you're also saying that you're no use to me.'

Dalton couldn't help but stare down the barrel of Walker's gun, but he closed his eyes a moment, then fixed his gaze on Walker's eyes.

'I'm not.'

'That's a foolish thing to say when you're staring down the barrel of my gun. So you got one last chance.' Walker firmed his gun hand. 'Tell me!'

Dalton stared deep into Walker's eyes. 'I don't know where the necklace is.'

'Then I believe you.' Walker grinned and thrust his gun arm out to its utmost, the arm rigid and the hand firm. 'And as a reward, you get to die.'

Walker searched Dalton's eyes, but Dalton just returned a firm gaze.

'Wait!' Milo shouted.

Walker glanced at Milo from the

corner of his eye.

'For what?'

'Dalton ain't got the necklace, but he knows where it is, and we can use him to get it.'

Walker breathed deeply through his nostrils, but then inch by inch lowered his gun.

'All right. I can postpone killing him for an hour.' He chuckled. 'But no longer.'

* * *

Once Deputy Hayden had tied Dalton's hands together, the lawmen mounted their horses and with Milo headed back to Harmony. The tethered Dalton trotted on behind them.

They maintained a slow enough pace that Dalton could avoid Hayden having to drag him into town, but fast enough that if he lost his footing even once, he would be lucky to regain his feet.

But at least the brisk journey warmed Dalton and dried his clothes.

Hayden and Vaughn glanced back frequently to belabour him with taunts that left him in no doubt that they were eager to remedy his escape the previous week from being dragged to death.

Walker rode up front, never once looking back at him.

Milo was now quieter. Dalton's revelation that they shared a common suffering at the hands of Misty subduing his previous thirst for revenge.

The sun was edging close to the horizon and shining through long swirls of deep red cloud as they rode into the church grounds.

Chase was outside the church, slamming a rifle butt against the door and yelling for Misty to come out, but when he saw Walker and the others riding towards him, he flinched back. He glanced left and right, then hurled the rifle to his shoulder.

Deputy Vaughn ripped his gun from its holster and his first shot winged the rifle from Chase's hand.

Chase feinted for the rifle, but as

another shot blasted into the ground inches from his questing hand, he danced back, then turned. He vaulted the low wall and hurtled down the road towards Harmony.

Vaughn broke into a gallop and even as Chase reached the first building on the outskirts of town, he closed on him. With a swirl of his arm, he freed a length of rope and at the first attempt lassoed Chase around the midriff.

Chase fell to his knees, then bounced along the road as Vaughn pulled his horse to a halt. Vaughn waited a moment for Chase to climb to his feet, then trotted back to the church with Chase stumbling on behind him.

At the church, Patrick swung the door open and peered outside. He glanced at the trussed Chase, then at Dalton. He winced but then looked up at Walker with a firm gaze.

'Thank you for helping us,' he shouted as he edged outside and closed the door behind him. 'Chase was all set on causing trouble.'

Walker nodded. 'Where's Misty Valdez?'

'She's praying for deliverance from Chase's wrath.'

'Get her out here.'

Patrick smiled. 'Perhaps when you've taken Chase away, she might feel safe enough to come out.'

Walker slammed his fist on his saddle.

'Get her out here,' he roared, spit flying from his mouth, 'or I'll drag her out.'

'You cannot — '

Misty emerged from the church and laid a hand on Patrick's shoulder, silencing him. She glanced at Chase, shivered, then looked up at Walker.

'Thank you, Sheriff,' she said, 'for arresting Chase.'

'I ain't arrested him,' Walker grunted with a smirk. 'I'm just preparing to question him. But you might save me the trouble.'

Misty took a long pace towards Walker. 'I'll answer anything.'

'You know what I want.' Walker

widened his eyes. 'The ruby necklace.'

Misty sighed. 'As Chase told you before, I have no ruby necklace.'

'That's a lie,' Milo shouted. 'I saw it.'

Misty glanced at Milo, her lips curled with distaste.

'Then you were mistaken.' She snorted and pointed at Chase. 'If I was rich enough to own something like that, do you think I'd be married to that . . . that pig?'

Walker glanced at Chase, who stood bowed and hunched, his flabby belly dangling, his jowls plastered to his neck.

'You have a point. He doesn't seem much of a husband for a woman like you.' Walker turned in the saddle to stare at Milo. 'What you got to say to that, Milo?'

'She has it,' Milo muttered. 'Last month I saw her down by the gully. She wore the rubies around her neck and was dancin' in the moonlight so much that the rubies shone in her face.'

Misty snorted and with a contemptuous dart of her hand, ripped the wooden bead necklace from her neck and dangled it in her outstretched hand.

'Was this the necklace you saw?'

Milo narrowed his eyes. A momentary flash of something invaded his eyes, perhaps fear, before he blinked it away and pointed at the necklace, his finger trembling.

'It's sure like that wooden one, but this one was made of rubies.'

'The beads are polished. In the moonlight, they shine so brightly that it's easy to imagine they are rubies.' Misty rubbed the beads, her voice wistful. 'I do that myself sometimes, but in the morning when the light returns, they are just what they always were, wood.'

Walker urged his horse forward a pace and reached down to Misty for the necklace. She held on to them a moment, then passed them up to him.

Walker dismounted and stood tall, fingering the beads, then, with his face set in a deep scowl swirled round to face Milo, the beads thrust out and swaying in his outstretched hand.

'You'll be looking down the barrel of my gun any moment, Milo. So think before you answer.' Walker's right eye twitched. 'Did you see rubies or did you see wood?'

Milo gulped. 'I know what I saw. I know what I saw. I saw her dancin'. I saw a necklace around her neck. I saw the moonlight shinin' off those beads so brightly that they had to be rubies, not wood. That's what I saw.'

Walker held the necklace aloft. The rays of the low sun dragged a glint from the beads that hinted at the redness of precious stones.

'Could be a mistake,' he mused.

'It is,' Misty said. 'Milo got it wrong and these wooden beads do shine in the moonlight. About the only thing Chase and me ever agreed on is that Milo ain't that clever.'

'I can see that.' Walker shook the necklace at Misty, causing the beads to rattle. 'So you're saying these wooden beads shine so brightly in the moonlight that they light up your face?'

'They do.'

Walker glanced at the low sun, then at the halfmoon high in the sky and emerging from behind a swirl of wispy cloud. He grinned, then swung the beads round to gather them in a large hand.

'Then we just have to wait until it's good and dark.' Walker hurled the beads to Misty, a huge grin on his face. 'Then you get to dance in the moonlight and we can all see who's telling the truth.'

15

Walker let Patrick and Misty sit on the church steps.

With Milo's fate in the balance, Deputy Vaughn tied him up, then positioned him to sit back to back with Dalton.

Milo suffered the indignity with sullen indifference.

With a single loop of rope, Vaughn tied them together, then positioned Chase before a discarded wagon wheel. To keep all three men in view, he sat on the remnants of the stone church wall ten yards from them and roved his gaze between them with his jaw set firm and his gun rested on his knee. His posture suggested that even when so tied he expected them to mount an escape attempt at any moment.

Deputy Hayden stood guard between the church and Harmony, but why after all the trouble Walker had caused here they thought that someone might venture out of Harmony, Dalton didn't know.

Walker sat on a collapsed length of stone wall beside the church, a leg pulled up to place his knee by his shoulder and his eyes only for the sun, watching it creep nearer and nearer to the horizon.

From time to time, Dalton glanced towards the church, trying to meet Patrick's or Misty's sullen gaze, but they both kept their heads down.

Dalton relented from watching everyone around him and sat tall, relaxing as much as he could, hoping that he might find some give in the bonds.

But even when he drew his chest in as much as he could, the ropes still cut into his skin. He relented, but when Vaughn rolled to his feet and sauntered in a circle, stretching his legs, he squirmed, attempting to force the ropes to slip down his chest.

Milo nudged an elbow into his back.

'Quit tryin' to escape,' he grunted.

'Just getting comfortable,' Dalton said.

'You'll get all the comfortable time you want soon enough.' Milo chuckled. 'Provided Walker buries you.'

'Stop trying to taunt me.' Dalton relented from his squirming, then leaned back to rest the back of his head on Milo's shoulder. 'But tell me one thing, will those beads shine?'

For long moments Milo didn't reply. Then he sighed and leaned back.

'Why do you ask?'

'Because I'd just like to know what Walker's reaction will be.'

Milo snorted a humourless laugh. 'What good will that do you? You'll end up dead no matter what happens.'

'Perhaps, but I just want what you want. I want to get out of this alive and if I know what Walker will do when Misty dances, I can work out how to do that.'

Milo rolled his shoulders, then sat tall. 'You know they won't shine. You've seen the ruby necklace, just like me.'

'You're wrong. So I ask again, are you sure those wooden beads won't shine like rubies?'

'I'm stakin' my life on it.'

'You are.' Dalton snorted. 'But perhaps I misjudged you.'

'What . . . ' Milo lowered his head when Vaughn's sauntering closed on him and with a glare told him to quieten.

Dalton leaned back, content to let the enforced silence work on Milo's mind.

He reckoned another thirty minutes passed before Vaughn stood again and stretched his legs, taking in a slow walk around Chase in the process.

Milo sighed. 'What you mean by misjudgin' me?'

'I mean you spoke up for me. Walker was all set to kill me. Then you told him not to.'

'I didn't save you because I support you. I saved you because I reckoned you knew where the necklace is. And I used that information to buy my way out of trouble.'

'Then I pity you. Vaughn bound you just like he bound me, and Walker ain't letting anyone live to tell what happens here.' Dalton lowered his voice to a whisper. 'And I don't know about no necklace.'

Milo snorted. 'You do. I followed you and Santiago. I'm good at hidin' and I overheard your conversations. You were lookin' for the rubies.'

'You're right. I did listen to Santiago's story and it intrigued me. I worked for Chase so that I could search for the necklace. But I found no sign that it even existed in the first place, so I was just leaving town.'

'You wouldn't give up that easily. And Santiago was all set to leave town with you. And he wouldn't do that unless you'd found it.'

Dalton sat straight. 'You got me wrong.'

'And whether or not those beads shine, I reckon Walker will ask you that question again. And you'll tell him everythin' once he's worked on you, believe me.' As the last sliver of sun disappeared below the horizon and the light level dropped within seconds to a pallid dusk, Milo chuckled. 'Now quit talkin', Dalton. I ain't interested in your lies.'

Dalton struggled against his bonds, hoping that he could slam an elbow into Milo's back. But as he found no give in his bonds, he saved himself the effort and settled down.

Walker uncoiled himself from the wall and sauntered to Vaughn's side. They shared low words, but they occasionally raised their voices, perhaps deliberately, and from those snippets Dalton learned that Vaughn had heard a lot of his conversation with Milo, and neither he nor Vaughn believed Dalton.

For the next hour, Dalton relented from his efforts to persuade Milo to help him and Walker marched back and forth before the church, swaggering when he wandered past one of his captives. Every third or fourth journey, he glanced at the moon, then at the thinning arc of lighter sky on the western horizon.

As night spread, Milo's former sullenness disappeared and he started shuffling back and forth, even calling out to Walker to free him.

Only by straining his neck could Dalton see the church. Misty and Patrick still sat on the step. Both had their heads bowed, presumably in prayer, and from Misty's impassive demeanour, Dalton couldn't detect what she expected the result of her dancing would be.

Then Walker paced round to stand before the church door and ripped the necklace from his pocket.

'Misty,' he shouted, thrusting the necklace aloft. 'It's time for you to dance.'

16

Walker pointed a firm finger at Misty and gestured for her to stand before the church.

With a last glance at Patrick and an encouraging nod, to which Patrick just returned a blank stare, Misty took the necklace from Walker and wrapped it around her neck, then paraded out from the church.

She faced the moon and with her back straight and her chin aloft, she appeared calm. The moon's weak light lit her neck and chin, but if there was any reflection from the wooden beads, Dalton couldn't see it.

'Dance,' Walker muttered. 'Like you do when you reckon you're alone.'

Misty closed her eyes, taking long, deep breaths, her bosom rising and falling. Then she hoisted her skirts to knee level and kicked her shoes away.

She lifted a leg high, her foot pointed, her calf arched, then swirled on the spot, then pranced in a circle, then jumped, then pirouetted.

Dalton had seen saloon girls dance in the big cities, but Misty's dance was more natural, almost primal. She swirled and leapt, her skirts billowing around her, her arms arched in intricate patterns that somehow conveyed animals, and birds, and even jaunty music that from somewhere invaded Dalton's mind.

Lost in the moment of watching her, everyone stared agog, even Walker and Patrick, but then Milo shuffled against his bonds and screeched out, his voice ripping through the magic to return everyone to the moment.

'Those beads ain't shinin',' he whined, triumph in his voice. 'They just ain't shinin'.'

With a last clap of her hands above her head, Misty stopped her dance and slammed her hands on her hips as her skirts swung to a halt.

'You wouldn't have known what you saw when you spied on me,' she said, her chin held aloft. 'Your eyes would have only been on me, not what was round my neck. Unless you ain't any kind of man.'

Milo grunted his annoyance, then lowered his head to his chest.

Walker shrugged. 'You can captivate a man when you dance, but I reckon Milo gets more excited by the thought of money than by the sight of a woman. His eyes would have been on that necklace, not you.'

Misty shook the beads at him, her eyes wide and bright.

'And do they not shine like I said they would?'

'Your eyes shine. Your skin gleams. But those beads are just dull.'

Misty held the necklace out to its utmost and peered up at the moon, then down at the beads, seemingly looking for a hint of light. She shrugged and released the beads for them to swing down to her throat.

'And when did Milo see me dance?'

Walker glanced at Milo.

Milo shuffled up and rocked his head from side to side.

'Three weeks ago,' he murmured, 'maybe four.'

'Three weeks ago the moon was full and far brighter than that half-moon,' Misty muttered, pointing at the moon. 'In full moonlight the beads would have shone, but in this light, they can only hint at their glory.'

She shook the beads and for just a moment, a faint sparkle from the beads rippled across her features.

'So to prove who's lying,' Walker grunted, 'we just have to wait another week?'

Misty nodded. 'I will dance for you again when the moon is full, if that is what you want.'

Walker snorted. 'I ain't got that much patience. I want the ruby necklace *now*.'

'You can only have these wooden beads. It is the only necklace I own.'

Walker glared at her, but as she returned his gaze, Hayden sauntered round to join him.

'She can dance by firelight,' Hayden said. 'That'll be the same as moonlight.'

Misty snorted. 'The moon is above me. A fire would be below me.'

'It will be all around you,' Walker said, 'if I say it will.'

Walker stalked to her side and lunged for the necklace.

Misty danced back from him, Walker's lunge closing on air. But with a defiant smile, she unhooked the necklace and held it out.

Walker snatched the beads from her and joined Hayden, who lit a brand. They hunched over the necklace and darted their gazes from the beads to the fire.

Then Walker swirled away and hurled the necklace at Misty for it to slam into her chest and slip to the ground.

'I have had enough of these guessing games,' he roared.

Misty provided a thin smile. 'They

shone, didn't they?'

'Yeah, but anything looks bright by firelight and I trust one thing more than I trust the light.' Walker pointed at Milo and Dalton. 'I trust liars and thieves like Milo and Santiago and Dalton. Those men reckoned you had a ruby necklace and they risked their lives to get it. So there is a second necklace and that one has rubies. And you'll give it to me.'

Misty slumped to the ground to grab the necklace and when she jumped to her feet, she held them in an outstretched hand, presenting the wooden beads to Walker.

'I can only give you these wooden beads.' She swung the beads round and round her index finger, then darted her hand down for them to fly from her hand and hurtle past Walker's nose. 'And in a week, when they shine by the full moon, you'll regret whatever it is you're planning to do.'

Walker glanced back at the discarded necklace, then turned and licked his lips.

'You're wrong. Either I get the rubies or I don't, but either way plenty of people are about to die. So tell me where they are and those people get to live.'

'There are no rubies.'

Walker stared at her a moment, then shrugged and backed a pace. He grabbed the beads and bunched them in his hand, then strode to Chase's side, swinging a stray tangle of beads from side to side.

'And what about you?' he said. 'Do you still say there are no rubies?'

Chase kicked at the earth, then looked up, his face set in a deep sneer.

'Misty never wears anything fancy. That's what I told you last week. That's what I'll tell you now. You're believing the deluded dreams of some idiot who used to work for me and couldn't take his eyes off my wife long enough to do no work.'

Walker glanced at Hayden. 'Tie him to the wheel.'

'I got nothing to say,' Chase muttered

as Hayden grabbed his arms.

'You didn't talk last week, but you were whining so much, I relented. This time, I ain't ever stopping.'

'I didn't talk last week because I had nothing to tell you.'

'Then you won't enjoy your last hour on Earth.' As Hayden secured Chase to the wheel with Vaughn's help, Walker sauntered to the church to stand before Patrick. 'Start praying, preacher man. Another sinner is about to have his Judgement Day.'

Patrick glanced at Chase, then lowered his head and murmured to himself.

'Don't,' Misty whispered.

Walker sneered. 'I thought you hated your pig of a husband?'

'I do. But this isn't right. Whatever he's done to me, he doesn't deserve this.'

'Don't worry.' Walker ordered Vaughn to hit Chase, then cracked his knuckles. 'Your turn will come soon and I'm keeping myself good and fresh for you.'

'Even you wouldn't kill a woman.'

Walker smirked as Vaughn's first blow thundered into Chase's guts, forcing Chase to splutter and screech.

'You're wrong, and while you watch Vaughn break every bone in Chase's body, it'll give you time to think.'

Misty winced and turned towards the church, but Walker took two long paces to loom over her, then grabbed her wrists and swung her round. With her back to him, he lifted her chin, forcing her to watch Vaughn thunder steady blows into Chase's flabby body.

Twenty yards from the group, Dalton leaned back to whisper to Milo.

'Do you think he'll kill him?'

'Kill Chase?' Milo snorted. 'Yeah, no trouble, no trouble at all.'

'Whatever Walker is, he's a lawman. He must have some belief in the law, no matter how misguided.'

'You're wrong. Chase is a mean varmint, and this just gives him an excuse to execute some summary justice.'

'Yeah, but when it comes to questioning Misty, surely he'll show some decency.'

'Nobody's ever called Walker decent. But don't worry about her. She's the most valuable person here. Walker will let Vaughn and Hayden loose on you long before he starts work on her.' Milo giggled. 'So tell Walker where those rubies are and save yourself a whole lot of pain.'

Dalton sighed. 'So, no matter what I say to you, you'll still reckon I know where they are?'

'Yep.'

Dalton leaned his head back so that the back of his head was lying on Milo's shoulder. As another blow from Vaughn smashed into Chase's jaw, knocking his head to the side, Dalton lowered his voice to a whisper.

'Then you're right. I do know where they are.'

Milo stiffened, then uttered a low chuckle.

'I knew it,' he gibbered. 'I just knew it.'

'Yeah. You were right.' Dalton lowered his voice even more forcing Milo to stop his gibbering to hear him. 'But, Milo, I've been thinking. Walker doesn't have to be the one who gets them.'

17

Milo uttered a low whistle as Hayden took over from Vaughn and crunched his first blow into Chase's jaw, snapping his head back against the wheel.

Milo breathed deeply through his nostrils, but then shuffled back to lean against Dalton.

'Seems you've spent so much time with Santiago that you reckon you can bargain your way out of anythin'. But it didn't work for Santiago and it won't work for you.'

'Perhaps what Santiago had to bargain with wasn't as enticing as what I have.'

For long moment Milo muttered to himself.

'All right,' he whispered. 'What you offerin'?'

'A joint share.'

'An interestin' offer. But you ain't

temptin' me. Walker's offerin' somethin' I like even more than rubies — my life.'

Dalton snorted and gestured with his head towards Hayden, who rolled his shoulders then rained a flurry of blows into Chase's body.

'Yeah, but do you reckon Walker will let you live once he has them?'

'Don't see why not.'

'Then you're even more stupid than I thought. Walker's already killed Santiago. He won't let any witnesses to what happens here live.'

'I don't believe that. Walker ain't a good lawman, but he likes people who prove their worth to him. And after tonight I reckon I can do anythin' I like in Harmony. I might even declare myself mayor. And everyone will have to respect me.'

Dalton looked upwards, keeping silent and letting the steady smack of fist against flesh wash over them both.

'If you want respect, being Walker's puppet won't provide that. As soon as you annoy him, he'll kill you. But if you join me, I reckon those rubies will buy you every ounce of respect you could ever want, and all on your terms, not Walker's.'

'I ain't interested.'

'I'll take all the risks. Your part ain't dangerous.'

Dalton silenced as Chase let rip with a loud screech, followed by a babbling plea to Walker to relent, but Walker just feigned a yawn and ordered Hayden to resume beating him.

'What part?'

'Bring Santiago's horse and gun to the gully behind the church while I talk my way into getting free long enough to collect the rubies.'

'How?'

'That ain't your concern. But I ask you again — do you want half the rubies or do you want to be Walker's puppet?'

Milo hung his head. But a louder than usual crack echoed as Hayden slammed a long backhanded slap to

Chase's cheek, and he coughed.

'Hey, Walker,' he shouted. 'How much longer do I have to stay tied to Dalton's smelly hide?'

Walker pushed Misty to Vaughn and sauntered towards Milo and Dalton.

'Until I say so,' he said.

'But I was right about Misty,' Milo whined. 'Those beads didn't shine. So you know she has another necklace now. And I ain't no use to you any more.'

'Suppose you ain't. But then again I can't see you ever being any use to anyone.' Walker narrowed his eyes. 'So where will you go?'

'As I ain't gettin' a share in the rubies and Santiago ain't got any use for those horses, I could head out and claim them.'

Walker sneered but then gestured for Hayden to untie him.

As the rope pooled around his feet, Milo rubbed his wrists.

Then, without even a glance at Dalton, he scurried away and mounted his horse. With his gaze set forward, he trotted away from the church and towards the gully.

As Milo disappeared into the gloom, in an unbidden gesture, Dalton crossed his fingers behind his back, hoping that the untrustworthy Milo was helping him after all, then coughed.

'What about me?' he shouted.

'You ain't going after Milo,' Walker said with a snort. 'Once Vaughn and Hayden have finished with Chase, they'll question you.'

'I thought you'd say that.' Dalton placed a resigned smile on his face. 'So can I head into the church first?'

'Why?'

'To share my last words with God.'

'You don't want to do that. You have a pathetic plan to escape.'

'As I can't tell you where the rubies are, you'll kill me. And even I have something I need to say before that.'

Walker grunted his disbelief, but Patrick dashed from the church to stand beside him.

'Please,' he said, his hands clasped and pleading. 'You have inflicted intolerable cruelty on others, but you can't deny a man's immortal soul a chance of redemption.'

'The likes of Dalton has an immortal soul?' Walker chuckled. 'Then who am I to threaten that?'

'Thank you.'

With a firm lunge Walker grabbed Patrick's collar and pulled him up close.

'I got no intention of hurting you, preacher man, but if while you're tending to Dalton's immortal soul, you help him escape, I'll give your immortal soul plenty to think about.'

Walker held on to Patrick's collar a moment longer, then hurled him to the ground. He stalked back to the wheel, but with a flick of his wrist, he ordered Hayden to release Dalton.

Hayden unwound the rope from Dalton, then dragged him to his feet and pushed him towards the church.

Dalton stretched his tired limbs, then

walked tall with Patrick at his side, but as he passed Misty, he flashed a look at her, then at the church. She turned away, but as she did, her chin had returned to its previous defiant angle.

Dalton entered the church and paced down the aisle, but he stopped halfway along and turned.

'For this,' Patrick said, 'we should be by the altar.'

'I'm sorry, Patrick,' Dalton said. 'I ain't interested in you saving my immortal soul. I just wanted to get in here.'

'Dalton, don't do anything to make things worse.'

'Things can't get any worse.' Dalton hung his head a moment. 'But whatever I'm planning to do, I won't get you killed. Don't worry about that.'

'I wasn't worried about that. But I still hope we can end this with nobody dying.'

'I'd settle for that too. And to do that I need to talk to Misty.'

'She's outside.'

'Yeah. But not for — '

The church door slammed open and Walker hurled Misty inside. She wheeled to a halt, then swirled round to glare back at him, but already Walker was slamming the door shut.

She glared at the closed door, then swirled round to face Dalton and placed a grim smile on her lips.

'Why did you want me to come in here?' she asked.

'To ask you to speak up about the rubies,' Dalton said.

'I can't. There are no rubies.'

'But you . . . ' Dalton sighed and glanced at Patrick, then shrugged. 'I need to talk to her in private.'

Dalton gave Patrick no time to argue and instead grabbed Misty's arm and led her down the aisle then into Patrick's room. There, he closed the door and leaned back against the wall beside Patrick's bedding, and the location of the hidden necklace, then turned to her.

Misty stood beside the door with her chin held high.

'Dalton, I have nothing to say to you that I can't say in front of Patrick.'

'Even about your promise to give me the necklace if I killed Chase?'

Misty hung her head. 'Perhaps not about that. But believe me now — I lied to you that I had a ruby necklace. And I'm sorry, Dalton. But I was desperate. I had to do something to stop Chase beating me.'

'So you offered me something that doesn't exist to kill your husband, just like you offered yourself to Milo?'

Misty glanced away, gulping. 'I'm not proud of that. But I had no choice.'

'And what about Patrick? What did you offer him?'

Misty swirled back to face him, her jaw clenched in what Dalton took to be righteous indignation.

'Nothing. I have only sought spiritual help from him. And I help him in ways you wouldn't understand.'

'Why? You don't believe in Patrick's message.'

'I need solace from Chase. And if you

or Milo had done as I asked, I needed to atone for my sins.'

'You're saying you planned to seek redemption after you'd organized someone to kill Chase?'

'That was my plan.'

'I ain't no religious type, but I don't reckon it works like that.'

Misty slammed her arms into a folded position.

'You can't judge me.'

'I can't. But I reckon that atonement can start now. Head outside and tell Walker where the rubies are.'

Misty winced so deeply a tear escaped her right eye.

'I'm getting tired of saying this today, but there are no rubies.'

'There are,' Dalton snapped. He rubbed at his forehead as he considered Misty, but as she glanced away from him, a momentary flash of indecision flickering in her eyes, he nodded. 'But that was your plan all along, wasn't it? You've pushed everyone until Walker is so convinced they exist, he'll kill Chase.

Then, when he's dead, you'll tell Walker where they are to save your own hide.'

Misty edged back a pace to bump into the wall.

'You're wrong.'

'I'm not. But don't think I'll go quietly. I'll tell Patrick. He's put his faith in me and I reckon he's put his faith in you too. I reckon he already suspects I'm not worthy, but he deserves to know who you are.'

'He'll forgive me.'

'Don't risk that. Deliver on his faith the right way. Tell Walker now where the rubies are and stop him killing Chase.'

'I am not doing that.'

'Then go outside and watch him kill your husband.' Dalton dashed to her side, grabbed her arm, and pushed her towards the door. 'See whether you can stomach that.'

Misty glared back at Dalton, her chin high and defiant.

'There's more here at stake than you know.'

'I feel sorry for your predicament — no man can hit a woman — but you can find a solution that doesn't lead to Chase dying.'

'You don't know enough about what I've gone through and what I want to happen here to judge me.' She shrugged from Dalton's grip, but still opened the door. She glanced outside, then turned back and lowered her voice to a whisper. 'But please believe this — do nothing and say nothing, Dalton. I'm doing it all for Patrick. My life doesn't matter.'

Dalton grabbed the door and pushed her outside, then slammed the door shut behind her. He listened, hearing Patrick ask her what had happened. From the low sob Misty returned him, Dalton reckoned that she'd be relaying her lies for a while yet, so he dashed to the bedding and knelt.

Working frantically he shovelled straw, then earth away until he'd revealed the loose stone. He jabbed his fingers into the gap and prised it from the wall, then pulled the box out, clutching it to his chest before he set it on the ground.

Inside, something heavy rattled.

Dalton took a deep breath and fingered the delicate lock, but then outside, he heard two sets of footfalls pace towards the church door.

He looked to the roof a moment, offering his own silent prayer for sufficient time, but out in the church, the door slammed shut and footsteps, presumably Patrick's, paced back down the aisle.

Dalton wavered a moment, but as he didn't have enough time to replace the box and this would be his last chance to retrieve the necklace, he sprang the lock and swung back the lid.

Dalton rolled back on to his haunches, his surprise paralysing him.

The box didn't contain a necklace.

But it did contain a gunbelt and Peacemaker.

In one hand Dalton hefted the belt and whistled under his breath.

Behind him the door creaked open,

but he was still so bemused that he just swung the gunbelt back and forth.

'So, Dalton,' Patrick said, pacing through the door. 'Is that not what you expected to find?'

18

'Whose belt is this?' Dalton snapped, swirling round to face Patrick.

'Mine.'

'And why hide it in here?'

Patrick swung the door back and forth, his gaze seemingly not for this time or place.

'It is my shame. I was once a man not unlike Walker, perhaps not unlike you. I can't forget who I was and what I did.' Patrick held out his hand. 'But that is not important now. Give it to me.'

'I ain't lying to you. I hoped this would be the ruby necklace. But seeing as it ain't, I'll settle for using a gun to get out of here.'

Patrick slammed the door shut with a resounding crash. He stood before the door with his hands on his hips, a firm-jawed gaze replacing his usual pious smile.

'If you strap on that gun, I'll kill you.' Patrick raised his hands and for the first time, Dalton noticed how wide they were.

'You're a man of God. You wouldn't do that.'

'If you knew the man I was before I donned this robe, you wouldn't risk disobeying me.' Patrick took three steady paces towards Dalton, then stretched out a hand, palm up. 'Give me the gunbelt.'

Dalton shrugged, then moved to wrap the belt around his waist, but with a rapid swirl of his arm, Patrick swiped the belt from Dalton's grip and with a flick of the wrist clipped Dalton under the chin. The effortless blow knocked Dalton back two paces.

Dalton shook his head. 'You don't need to do this.'

Patrick looped the belt over his shoulder. 'I prayed to save Chase. I prayed to save Misty. I prayed to save you. None of that worked. Now I need to use the only way that'll work, the way

I was all set to use on the day you walked into my church — the way of the gun.'

'You got no need to save my life.'

'I don't care about you, not any more. So leave before I kill you too.'

'This ain't you talking.'

'It is.' Patrick snorted. 'I hoped you'd built that annex because a sprout of goodness had taken root in your soul. I hoped it wasn't guilt, but it was something worse, you just wanted that necklace.'

'I did.' Dalton folded his arms. 'And what of it?'

'I put my faith in you, but you made all the wrong choices and now my deal with God is over.' Patrick sneered. 'Just get out of my sight! And this time, don't come back.'

Patrick threw open the door, grabbed Dalton's shoulder in a vice-like grip, and pointed into the church.

'Believe me when I say I didn't mean to destroy your faith.'

'Quit lying. You aimed to escape

down the tunnel and leave Misty and me to die.'

'I didn't. I told Misty to tell Walker about the necklace. Walker would have come after me and left you all alone — '

'Be quiet. A man like you only thinks of himself.' Patrick pointed through the door. 'So leave now or risk getting caught in the cross-fire.'

'But I . . . ' Dalton gulped down his last shred of dignity. 'All right.'

Patrick snorted and in sullen silence led Dalton through the church and into the room opposite. With a single tug, he pulled back the cupboard.

'Keep going,' Patrick said, his voice low and hurt. 'Don't look back no matter what you hear.'

Patrick turned and strode into the church, dismissing Dalton with a firm swirl of his robes.

Through the open door Dalton watched Patrick kneel before the cross and set the gunbelt before him, then place his head to the ground and begin a low murmuring, but he raised a fist and shook it at the cross.

With no pride in his actions, Dalton lifted the door and paced down the steps, along the tunnel and out the other side.

He sat on the topmost step, his disgust in himself bowing his head.

From the front of the church Chase's weak cries pierced the night air. But with his head still down Dalton jumped to his feet and scurried to the gully, then ran down it as quickly as he dared in the poor light. At his sides the banks were a lighter swathe against the star-filled blackness of night, the gully bottom an inky void.

At every pace he expected gunfire to blast out from behind him, but it didn't come and neither did his disgust in his actions lighten.

He judged that he'd run for a mile when he paused for breath and on hands and knees climbed from the gully. On cresting the top, two hundred yards ahead, a rider was silhouetted against the night sky, heading towards him along the top of the bank. A second horse trotted along behind.

Dalton jumped on the spot and waved towards the rider, but although the rider was Milo, he continued at his same sedate pace. Dalton bit back his annoyance and waited.

'Hurry up,' he shouted when Milo was twenty yards away.

'Did you get it?' Milo asked, slowing to a halt ten yards before him.

'Just give me my gun and my horse.'

'Once I see the rubies.'

'You saying you don't trust me?'

Milo hunched forward in the saddle, his hand resting on a fold of fat above his gunbelt, his grin a slash of white in the dark.

'Nope, but the way I see it — I could just kill you and search your body. And as I ain't done that, you can trust me enough to show me the necklace.'

'Then if we're being all trusting towards each other, I'll tell you the truth. I don't have it.'

Milo grunted. 'You'd better not be jestin' me.'

'I wish I were,' Dalton murmured.

Milo slapped his hand against his thigh, then urged his horse on to stand looking down at Dalton.

'But you said you knew where it was.'

'I did. The church was the only place Misty went outside her home. And I found this box in a secret hole in the wall. I thought the necklace was in there. But it was just Patrick's . . . his personal possessions.'

'So you're now claimin' again that you have no idea where it is?'

'Yep.'

'Then you don't get your horse and you don't get a gun.'

Milo dragged his gun from its holster then dismounted and, with his gun aimed at Dalton chest, paced to his side. He ordered him to hold his hands high, then patted his jacket. He ran his hands over every inch of Dalton's clothes working down to his boots, which he made him remove. Still he fingered inside them, then restarted the process.

'You've searched me,' Dalton murmured. 'Now give me my gun. You got nothing to lose. Walker won't know you helped me escape, and if he finds me, I ain't telling him.'

'Perhaps you've hidden the rubies somewhere.' Milo gulped. 'But if they're on you, I don't like to think where you've hidden them.'

'I ain't got them. I'm heading out of Harmony and I ain't returning.'

Milo stood back, his gun rested in the crook of his elbow.

'All right. I'll trust you enough to give you the horse, but not the gun.'

Dalton blew out his cheeks, but then nodded and wandered past Milo to mount the spare horse.

'Obliged,' he said when he'd righted himself in the saddle. 'But from the amount of trouble I'll face when Walker comes after me, I need a gun.'

Milo shook his head and mounted his horse.

'No way. You just get to do what you said you'd do, and leave. And don't argue no more. You're startin' to irritate me.'

Dalton moved his horse on a pace, but then swung it to the side to stand alongside Milo.

'The gun, Milo.'

Milo glared at Dalton, then swung his gun round to aim it at him, but before he could blast off a shot, Dalton leaned from the saddle and with a flailing arm, clipped Milo's shoulder, knocking him to the side.

As Milo fought to right himself, Dalton stood in the saddle and hurled himself at Milo. His foot caught as he leapt and he only bundled into Milo. Even so he tumbled him from his horse and the two men crashed to the ground and rolled over each other, entangled.

Milo swung his gun in, trying to aim it at Dalton's chest, but Dalton grabbed a firm grip of his arm and thrust his hand high above his head. He swung the arm back and forth, until he shook the gun from Milo's grip.

The gun swirled end over end before it crashed into the dirt, both men pausing from their tussle to watch it land. Then they rolled to their feet and slugged blows at each other. From so close the blows landed with little force, but Milo darted his head forward in an attempted head butt.

Dalton saw the blow coming and ripped his head back, the blow only slamming into his chin, and it was Milo who staggered back stunned. Taking this as his chance, Dalton took a long rolling dive at the gun. As he rolled over the gun he struggled it into his grip and kept the roll going. Only when he slid to a halt did he slip round to lie flat on his belly.

Milo had shook off his ill-timed head butt and was dashing towards him, but Dalton slammed his elbows into the ground, gaining a firm triangle, and aimed the gun up at Milo.

With a resigned grunt, Milo slid to a halt and raised his hands.

'You double-crossing varmint,' he muttered.

'I won't shoot you,' Dalton said, keeping his voice calm. 'I just aim to leave here alive. And I need this gun. So give me the gunbelt and this is over.'

Milo glared at him, but then unhooked the belt and hurled it to Dalton's feet.

'You won't get away with that necklace. I'll track you down.'

'Milo, you couldn't track down your own feet.' Dalton beckoned Milo to back ten paces, then jumped to his feet and wrapped the belt around his waist. He holstered his gun and walked sideways to his horse and, with his gaze still set on Milo, mounted it. 'But save yourself the trouble. I'm not leaving town with the necklace.'

Dalton swung the reins to the side, turning his horse towards Harmony.

'If you're tellin' the truth, why ain't you headin' out of Harmony?'

'I ain't got to explain myself to you.' Dalton raised the reins, then lowered them. 'But if you have an ounce of sense, stay out of Harmony for the next hour and you might just live.'

Milo narrowed his eyes. 'If you're headin' back to Harmony to try to save Misty, you're wastin' your life on her.'

'I never asked your opinion, but you're right. She ain't worth saving. But I'm returning to save something more important than rubies or a woman or even my own dignity.' Dalton hurried his horse on towards Harmony. 'I have to save Patrick's immortal soul.'

19

With every pace that Dalton galloped back to Harmony, he expected to hear gunfire ripping out from ahead as Patrick burst from the church.

But only silence greeted him.

So he risked a more cautious approach and headed in a long arc from the gully. He swung round to the front of the church, approaching at a steady trot with his gaze set towards Harmony.

Walker turned to face him, but Dalton reckoned in the poor light he wouldn't recognize him, and he guessed that of all the things he expected to see, Dalton riding back towards him wasn't one of them.

Even so, he turned his hat towards the church to mask his features, but from the corner of his eye, he saw that Hayden relented in his beating of Chase to watch his approach. But

Chase lay slumped against his bonds, seemingly beyond the ability to care that the beatings had stopped.

Walker and Vaughn swung round to face him. On the church steps, Misty looked at him, only her rigid posture suggesting that she recognized him.

Patrick wasn't outside.

'Keep riding by,' Walker shouted when Dalton was beside the church.

Dalton kept his face set forward and paced his horse past the church, but just as Walker gestured to Hayden to resume his assault of Chase, Dalton swung his gun from its holster and pulled his horse to a halt.

'Untie Chase,' he shouted.

Walker flinched, then swirled round to face Dalton, but it was only to stare down the barrel of his gun.

As Dalton's aim wasn't as sure as he sometimes liked to think it was, from thirty yards away, Walker stood a good chance of surviving, but with a shrug, Walker gestured for Vaughn to release Chase from the wheel.

With a few swift gestures, Vaughn ripped the ropes from Chase's form, letting Chase slump, boneless, to the ground.

'What you want, Dalton?' Walker shouted.

Dalton swung his horse around and with a tight rein paced towards the church. He slipped through a collapsed length of wall and halted ten yards before the church door.

'I want you to leave everyone alone.'

'That ain't happening.'

'Then we got ourselves a problem because I don't want to kill you.'

Walker rolled his shoulders and stood firm. On either side of him, Vaughn and Hayden shuffled round to face Dalton with smug grins plastered across their firm-jawed faces. They settled down and dangled their hands beside their holsters.

Dalton glanced at the church door, but as he turned his gaze back on Walker, Chase staggered to his feet and half-threw, half-collapsed himself on top of Vaughn, bundling him to the ground.

As Walker and Hayden swirled on the hip to train their guns on the entangled twosome, Dalton jumped to the ground. Walker swung round, blasting a shot at him with his other arm held rigid above the gun, but the shot winged past Dalton's back as he hurled himself behind the church wall.

Walker and Hayden hunkered down. Walker faced the church wall. Hayden faced the battling Chase and Vaughn.

Dalton glanced up to see Vaughn squirm out from beneath Chase and club him away. Dalton blasted at him, but the shot was wild and with a contemptuous flick of the wrist, Vaughn ripped a shot into Chase's forehead.

Chase collapsed, soundless, to the ground.

From the church steps, Misty had the grace to screech and throw a hand to her mouth, but then she swirled round and dashed into the church, calling for Patrick and leaving the door open.

Dalton fired a speculative shot at Walker, then ducked. He stayed down to the count of five and swung up again but it was only to see Vaughn pounding down the side of the church wall towards him.

Dalton just had time to blast off a wild shot. Then Vaughn slammed into him, knocking him to the ground. They tumbled over each other. Both men had a death grip on their guns and one-handed they wrestled each other's gun hands above their heads. But Vaughn was larger and his grip more powerful and with seeming ease, he dragged Dalton to his feet.

Dalton planted his feet wide and ensured he stayed facing the church, but inch by inch Vaughn dragged Dalton round.

Fifteen yards before him, Walker and Hayden both trained their guns on him, ready to fire the moment Vaughn gained them a clear shot.

A gunshot blasted nearby. Dalton winced, but to his surprise, Vaughn collapsed from his grip. Dalton hurled himself to the ground to hide behind the wall, amazed that Walker's aim had been so poor, but then another shot blasted and it came from beside him.

He glanced over his shoulder to see Milo galloping straight for the church.

Dalton swung his gun up on to the wall and blasted covering gunfire, forcing Walker and Hayden to seek cover behind the wall too.

Milo's horse skidded to a halt before the church, rearing as Milo pulled it round. Milo ripped a shot at Walker's position, then jumped down to join Dalton.

'Mighty glad to see you,' Dalton said. 'But why?'

'I ain't here to help you,' Milo grunted.

'You ain't still dreaming of that necklace are you? Because nobody is getting that, if it exists, today.'

'Maybe I am still dreamin'.' Milo sighed. 'But it ain't that. You were right. I can't hide from Walker for ever and this is my best chance to get some respect.'

Dalton nodded. 'Don't care what your motives are. I'm just happy that you're here.'

And with the extent of their partnership defined, they settled down on either side of the wall.

'You had enough, Walker?' Dalton shouted as he reloaded.

'Go to hell,' Walker shouted.

'You are going to hell,' a level voice said from the church doorway.

Dalton lifted to look at the church. Framed in the doorway stood Patrick. His robes were gone and on his hip, the Peacemaker gleamed.

'What you doing, preacher man?' Walker shouted.

Patrick flashed a smile and held his arm to the side.

'I'm inviting you into my church before you get to rot in hell.'

'I meant about that gun at your hip.'

'Thought the gun would be all you'd understand. Now come in here and we can end this.'

Patrick turned and stalked into the church. His form disappeared but his long shadow cast by an oil-lamp still darkened the church steps.

Walker muttered orders to Hayden, then doubled over dashed to the church. Behind him, Hayden ripped out covering gunfire at Chase and Milo, forcing them to duck, and when Dalton risked looking again, Walker was dashing into the church and Hayden was backing towards the door too.

But Hayden hunkered down beside the church doorway, sheltering in the lee of Dalton's annex.

'What is the preacher doing?' Milo asked.

'Going to hell too,' Dalton murmured. 'Cover me.'

Dalton slammed his gun into its holster and, not waiting for Milo to agree to his order, vaulted the wall. With his head down, he charged Hayden.

Milo's gunfire peppered the church wall, forcing Hayden to hide behind the annex wall as Dalton dashed for the church. But when Milo had blasted six shots Hayden leapt out from the annex, but it was only to walk into Dalton's thundering blow to the jaw.

Hayden shrugged off the blow, but Dalton followed through with a right cross that crunched into Hayden's chin and slammed his head back against the church wall.

As Hayden slumped to the ground, Dalton glanced over his shoulder, signifying with a click of his fingers that Milo should guard Hayden, then charged through the doorway and into the church, skidding on the ground in his haste.

But as he slid to a halt he saw that Walker had already turned on him, his gun aimed at his head and his gun hand firm.

Before the altar Patrick stood hunched, his right hand dangling inches from his holstered gun.

'Stand to the side, Dalton,' Walker muttered. 'You get to see the preacher man die before you die.'

Without a choice, Dalton raised his hands above his head and to Walker's directions joined Misty at the side of the church.

Misty looked at him, her cheeks colourless, her eyes wet, but Dalton didn't return her gaze as he tried to catch Patrick's eye.

But Patrick stood impassive, as much a statue as a man. Then, moving with extreme slowness, he raised his head to watch Walker swirl round to face him.

From five yards apart Patrick and Walker stared at each other, and in Dalton's view a cold confidence festered in both men's eyes.

'Damn you to hell for all eternity!' Patrick roared.

'You'll get there first,' Walker muttered.

'Don't, Patrick,' Dalton shouted. 'This ain't your way.'

'Dalton's right,' Misty screeched. 'The way of the gun is Walker's way. The way of the cross is your way.'

'It was,' Patrick murmured. 'But today, I return one of the Devil's minions to the hell-hole from which he sprang.'

Walker's right eye twitched. Then he threw his hand to his holster, but in a move like lightning, Patrick ripped his gun from its holster. A single gunshot blasted, the sound deafening in the small church, and ripped into Walker's chest, knocking him back and around.

Walker staggered a pace, his left arm clutching his chest, but even as he collapsed to his knees, Patrick had already turned and threw himself flat before the altar, his hands thrown to his face, sobs racking his body.

Walker pressed his head to the ground. He keeled over on to his side. But just as a last tortured gasp escaped his lips, Dalton pulled his gun from its holster and ripped a gunshot into his chest, then another and another.

With each shot, Walker's lifeless body twitched.

Only when Dalton had blasted all his

remaining lead did Patrick jump to his feet and swirl round to face him.

'Stop that,' he shouted. 'He's dead.'

'I had no choice,' Dalton shouted, reloading with frantic haste as he peered at the prone Walker. 'He was going to kill you.'

'What? I'd already killed him.'

'You didn't.' Dalton mimed a shot skidding off his ribs with the flat of his hand. 'You only winged him. He was going to shoot you in the back.'

'Dalton, I hit what I aim at.'

'Perhaps you once hit what you aimed at. But you ain't lived with a gun for many, many years.' Dalton strode to Walker's side and kicked him over. With the toe of his boot, he pointed at a rip of cloth on his side. 'And you ain't been keeping those skills in tune.'

Patrick strode down the aisle, his brow furrowed, and glanced down at Walker. He shook his head.

'That isn't what happened. Once you have the skill, you don't lose it.'

'Then perhaps you haven't. Perhaps

the decency that's invaded your soul veered your aim.'

Patrick glanced at Misty. 'Is that what happened?'

Misty and Dalton shared a glance. Then she nodded.

'Yeah,' she said. 'It's like Dalton said. You didn't kill Walker Dodge. Dalton did.'

20

Patrick glanced up at the cross, mouthed a silent benediction, then followed Dalton as he wandered outside. He had nothing to say to a man who had just killed another man, even one as evil as Walker Dodge.

But Patrick guessed that his silence also resulted from his own shame at what he had so nearly done.

Either way, his failure to kill Walker had blasted away all the doubts that he had lived with for the last few months.

Before the church door, Milo was lying on his back, rubbing his jaw.

'Where's Hayden?' Dalton asked.

'Vaughn was only wounded,' Milo murmured. 'And he jumped me. Then he and Hayden ran off. Sorry, but I ain't cut out for this.'

'Some might say you ain't cut out for anything, Milo.' Dalton sighed. 'But I reckon they just ran because they were scared of you.'

As Milo beamed with pleasure, Patrick narrowed his eyes and peered into the darkness but saw nothing beyond the church confines.

'After you removed such a corrupt lawman,' he said, 'nobody in Harmony will say a word against you, but those deputies will probably get the word out about what you did. And their version might differ from the word of everyone here.'

'It might,' Dalton said, patting Milo's shoulder. 'But whatever lies they spin about me, with Milo defending everyone here, I reckon they won't dare return.'

'I can help you chase them down if you want,' Milo said. 'Seein' as how they escaped from me.'

'No. I had to kill Walker Dodge.' Dalton removed his gunbelt and hurled it to Milo. 'I got no desire to kill again.'

Milo nodded. 'Then I reckon as I'll check that Verna is safe.'

Milo swung the belt over his shoulder, then raised his chin and strode into town.

'Perhaps there is hope for Milo,' Patrick said, then turned to Dalton. 'And for you.'

'Perhaps. I'm just sorry that you put your faith into the wrong man.' Dalton glanced at Misty, but Misty looked away.

'That isn't determined yet, Dalton. Every night I will pray that you seek the right path.'

Dalton shrugged. 'Pray for those closer to you.'

'What do you mean?'

'It ain't my place to speak up about what happens between . . . put it this way — I'll worry about you as much as you worry about me.'

'There is no need. Not now.' Patrick smiled, then unhooked his gunbelt and held it out. 'But while you search for your path, take this. I won't need it any longer. I have found my path.'

'I don't need a . . . ' Dalton sighed

and took the gunbelt. He swung it round his waist then wandered past Chase's lifeless body and mounted his horse. He faced the dark plains beyond the church, but then turned to Misty.

'Good luck,' she whispered.

'Obliged,' Dalton said, his voice gruff. 'And now that Chase's dead, what will you do now?'

'I'll do the right thing,' she said. 'Don't worry about that.'

'Glad to hear it. Like I said to Chase, one day I might come back this way and I don't want to find that everything hasn't turned out right.'

'I understand.'

'And just so I know, do . . . ' Dalton glanced around, but on seeing that Milo was fifty yards away as he wandered into town, he turned back to Misty. 'Do you actually own a ruby necklace?'

Misty paced to the discarded wooden bead necklace and wrapped it around her neck.

'I only have the one necklace, Dalton.'

'So it doesn't exist.'

Misty lowered her head over the beads, counting them, then with an irritated slap of her palm against her thigh, rooted on the ground until she found a bead that had slipped from the necklace.

She held it up to the moonlight, finding the hole in the bead with which she could slot it on to the chain and, for a moment, something shone deep within the hole.

'Sometimes,' she said, 'the best hiding place is in plain sight.'

Dalton nodded. 'I'll remember that.'

Dalton tipped his hat, then headed to the gap in the church wall and on to the trail. He stopped and glanced down, possibly searching for the deputies' tracks, then turned his horse and trotted from Harmony, but whether he was following them or avoiding them, Patrick couldn't tell.

'You were right,' Misty said. 'You

didn't put your faith into the wrong man.'

'I will continue to pray that I haven't. Just as I will continue to pray that I didn't put it into the wrong . . . ' Patrick lowered his head.

'Don't be ashamed of that thought. I wouldn't have let Walker beat Chase to death. I'd have given him what he wanted.'

Patrick nodded. 'So you *were* telling Dalton that the rubies exist.'

Misty smiled and turned from the church.

'With Walker gone,' she mused, 'it might be a good time for you to build that orphanage. I've always thought it'd cost less than a ruby necklace.'

Patrick nodded. 'I hope so.'

She watched Dalton disappear into the gloom. 'But is there hope for a man who killed a lawman?'

'There is.' Patrick sighed and turned back to the church. 'But such a man has a long journey ahead of him.'

We do hope that you have enjoyed reading this large print book.

Did you know that all of our titles are available for purchase?

We publish a wide range of high quality large print books including:
Romances, Mysteries, Classics
General Fiction
Non Fiction and Westerns

Special interest titles available in large print are:
The Little Oxford Dictionary
Music Book, Song Book
Hymn Book, Service Book

Also available from us courtesy of Oxford University Press:
Young Readers' Dictionary
(large print edition)
Young Readers' Thesaurus
(large print edition)

For further information or a free brochure, please contact us at:
Ulverscroft Large Print Books Ltd.,
The Green, Bradgate Road, Anstey,
Leicester, LE7 7FU, England.
Tel: (00 44) **0116 236 4325**
Fax: (00 44) **0116 234 0205**

Other titles in the
Linford Western Library:

BAR 10 JUSTICE

Boyd Cassidy

Gene Adams sends some of his Bar 10 cowboys to assist the law in protecting his rancher neighbours, for outlaws have been rustling vast numbers of cattle. But the rustlers are far more deadly than Adams had suspected and they kill more than half of his men and the posse, including the sheriff. Unwilling to risk any more of his cowboys, Adams secretly forces the town to make him the new sheriff. And so it is that he heads alone into the Badlands. But does he have the remotest chance of defeating his foe?

AMBUSH IN DUST CREEK

Scott Connor

When Marshal Lincoln Hawk rode into the lawless town of Dust Creek his mission was to clean out its trigger-happy outlaws. Lincoln's deadly Peacemaker did just that, but some of the outlaws escaped. Years later, when Lincoln rides into Dust Creek again, the town seems to have been abandoned. But it hasn't. Mason Black and his outlaw band are waiting for him. From behind every broken window, Mason's guns are aimed at his head. To see another dawn, Lincoln must face a desperate battle for survival . . .

SILVER GULCH FEUD

Scott Connor

Yick Lee and Carter Lyle realize that they've picked the wrong day to start working for Lorne Wayne. For two years Lorne has feuded with Alistair Marriott over the ownership of the Silver Gulch mine. But now the mine's giant protection man, Abe Mountain, is hell-bent on ripping apart that feud by blasting into oblivion anyone who stands in his way. Lee and Carter battle to uncover buried truths about the mine. But can they succeed and Abe's guns be silenced?

RETURN OF THE VALKO KID

Michael D. George

Marshal Clem Everett is summoned to Austin by Governor Hyram Sloane to track down a gang of outlaws led by Black Bill Bodie. His mission is to recover a document Bodie has stolen. Bodie is the fastest draw alive and only the outlaw Valko Kid has any chance of beating Black Bill. Sloane agrees to pardon Valko if the pair can retrieve the document. Clem Everett and the Valko Kid set off after Bodie to face untold carnage in their quest.

BUSHWHACKER

Bill Morrison

When Hal Coburn returned from the Civil War, he hoped to resume his former peaceful life. Instead he found a homecoming of hostility and a dark memory that haunted the minds of all who looked at him. Justice and revenge are often hard to separate and where there is no help from the law only the gun can even the score. Bushwhacking seems a low way of searching for justice, the result can be as savage as war itself, as Hal was to discover.